finding charlie

a novel by

Katie O’Rourke

Also by Katie O'Rourke

Monsoon Season
A Long Thaw
Still Life
Blood & Water

For Sean, whose belief in me makes me think I can do anything.

part one - Olivia

1. Tuesday

It was the neighbor's dog that woke me.

The curtained window was outlined in sunlight. The thick fabric had been advertised as "black-out curtains", and perhaps they performed as such in New Hampshire or Ohio. But they were no match for the sun in Arizona; some things were simply too much to ask for. Even this early, there was no keeping the day outside.

Rick's arm was heavy across my chest, trapping me in the bed like a stupid metaphor for this relationship. As if I needed it underlined. Officially, we'd broken up three months ago. But, in that time, I'd managed to wake up this way more times than I wanted to count.

I pushed his arm off me, my anger at myself coming out as anger at him. He groaned and rolled over, smiling sleepily without opening his eyes. As he reached for me, I jumped out of bed.

"Gotta pee," I said, shutting myself in the bathroom. I sat on the toilet with my head in my hands.

This bathroom was the worst thing about the apartment. When I'd moved here a year ago, I'd been sure that the mildew smell was something I could get rid of easily. I was wrong. The small, rectangular window was painted shut, making for humid, unventilated showers. The linoleum flooring curled along the edge of the tub.

But what sold me on the place were the old wood floors and the exposed brick walls. It was one of seven units, on the end so it only shared one wall, with a private, shady back patio. I'd never known my neighbors before, but here I knew them all. I watered Mrs. Rosen's plants when she went to visit her daughter in Scottsdale. The landlady's son, Manny, lived next door. He did repairs and fed my cat whenever Rick and I went away for a weekend.

Rick had spent a weekend sanding and staining the scratched floors, something my landlady was more than happy to allow.

I flushed and went to the sink. There, Oscar was curled into a ball, looking like a sink-full of liquid fur. It'd be hard to tell one end from the other, except that I knew the brightest orange stripe was on his forehead. I imagined I could pull the stopper and he'd be sucked down the drain. He'd just started sleeping in the sink this week, a sign that the weather had shifted to summer, the longest season in Tucson. It occurred to me that I should bump up the cooler, but that would mean leaving the bathroom.

I'd dated Rick for six years before it became clear it wasn't going anywhere, whatever that meant. I think it meant that he wanted babies, and I didn't. He came from an unbroken home. Whether his parents liked each other was up for debate as far as I could tell, but they never fought in front of their children and they passed on the idea that this kind of life wasn't just possible; it's what you did. You settled down, popped out a few kids, worked like hell to put them through school and never took time to consider whether this was the life you wanted.

I didn't grow up that way. My parents fought in front of us all the time, until I was twelve, and my mom left. She did take a moment to consider whether this was the life she wanted and her decision was a definite no. There was no custody agreement or visitation; she was just gone. My dad was left to raise two daughters on his own. My sister Charlotte was only six.

I turned the shower on, locking the bathroom door in case Rick got any cute ideas.

He'd asked me to marry him once. I still wasn't sure how serious he'd been. We were in Vegas, walking by a wedding chapel, and he'd said something like: "Let's just do it!"

I'd laughed it off, said "Yeah, right," and pulled his arm, making him walk faster. Who knows what might have happened if I'd taken him up on it. That was about a year ago.

I closed my eyes under the water and hoped he'd be gone when I got out. We'd already had several versions of the awkward, "let's not do this again" conversation. It was depressing.

My first patient of the day was someone new. Paige Sullivan had been referred by her OBGYN for last trimester back pain. The first appointment always felt to me like a bad first date – the uneven asking of getting-to-know-you questions. My job made small talk necessary. It helped to get a sense of their daily lives beyond the description of the injury or illness that brought them to Desert Oasis

Physical Therapy. Sometimes, that was how you figured out what was really going on: the joint pains of the retiree having to do with his new sedentary lifestyle, the athlete whose fear of missing the season made her minimize her symptoms.

Small talk was easy in Tucson. How long have you lived here? How about this heat? People who knew me in my real life would be surprised. I claimed to be horrible at small talk. Though, to be honest, it was less that, more that I just didn't care for it. Small talk was like the Hallmark card of conversation; it filled obligatory space without getting personal. In a professional context, that was appropriate. In the real world, it was a complete waste of time.

I shared the room with five other therapists. We each had a little curtained off examining area for assessing client needs and talking confidentially. The rest of the room was divided into work spaces; two exercise bikes, parallel bars, treadmill. Paige didn't need any of the big equipment. She squatted on a balance ball and used the green resistance bands to stretch. I stood over her and did the counting.

In college, I'd done a rotation in a neurology clinic where you got to spend hours with a single patient. That way, you really got to know them, got to feel like you made a real difference in the practical routines of their daily lives: showering, dressing, meal preparation. Teaching someone how to safely transfer from a wheelchair to their bed or the toilet could be the difference between living independently and winding up in a nursing home. Here, we got fifty minutes a week until the insurance companies told us to stop. The Medicaid patients got fifteen visits a year, sometimes more if we could write convincing progress notes.

The day was busy. None of my appointments canceled so the schedule was packed. My last client of the day had been coming for several weeks. It had become clear within the first few visits that Mrs. Henderson wasn't doing her home exercises. You could tell which ones were lying: they'd smile and nod when you asked and then five minutes later, you'd prompt a certain position and they'd return a blank stare. Sometimes, they'd confess like a guilty fifth grader, but more often they'd maintain their story with such dedication it made me wonder what kind of authority they thought I had. When I'd first started, I used to call them out. These days, I let it go. Hey, it's your funeral, Mrs. Henderson. Literally.

It used to wear on me how useless it made me. If the one hour a week in my presence was the only work they did, they'd never get better. But it evened out. The basketball player with the knee injury in a rush to get back to the game, the girl with early stage MS determined to keep up her strength, the eighty-two year old post-stroke who wanted to pick up his grandkids again. These were the troupers who validated my existence.

My father was in the waiting room when I left for the day. He looked so out of place – my big, strong dad in a room of broken, old people – and I realized he'd never visited me at work before. As I got closer, I saw he hadn't shaved and he wasn't dressed for work, wearing jeans and a t-shirt that promoted a political candidate who had run and lost years ago.

"Dad?"

He looked up as though he'd forgotten where he was, lost in the pattern of the carpet. "Olivia."

He wasn't smiling to see me. I touched his arm. "What's wrong?" I felt like I was bending over him, a little boy cowering over a broken toy. But he was taller than me.

And then he stood up straighter and put his arm around me and was in charge again. I was relieved to be ushered out the *woosh* of the automatic door and into the warm evening air under his direction.

Once outside, in relative privacy, he stood me in front of him and gripped my upper arms. "Charlie's missing," he said, ripping the band-aid off.

"She's *what*?"

"She didn't come home last night. I can't reach her on her cell."

I let out the breath I'd been holding, smiled warmly, condescendingly. "Dad. She's nineteen. I'm sure she just stayed out with a friend. Maybe she turned off her phone."

He let go of my arms then. "That's what the police said."

"The *police*?"

"They aren't taking it seriously because, legally, she's an adult." He said "legally" like it was a made up word. Clearly, she wasn't *really* an adult. I tended to agree. "I'm not overreacting."

"I didn't say that. Look, let me try her." I shifted my messenger bag to the front and started digging.

"She's never stayed out overnight without calling."

"I know." Everything was a mess inside.

"*You* never did."

"I know." I felt something hard, but it was just my camera.

"It's not allowed."

I pulled my phone out and found her name at the top of my contact list. "I *know*."

"I have not laid eyes on her since yesterday morning. She was in bed when I left for work."

I had to admit I didn't like the sound of that. Or of the call going directly to voicemail. "Maybe her battery died?" I whispered. "Charlie. We're worried. Call home."

My dad sat on a bench. "I'm not overreacting," he said again.

I sat next to him. "Did she say where she was going last night?"

He shook his head. "I came home and her car was gone. I looked for a note, texted her before I went to bed. Nothing. And now it's five o'clock. I have not seen or heard from your sister in thirty-three hours!"

"Did you try Carmen?" Charlie and Carmen had been best friends since first grade.

"I called the Rodriguez house all day. I kept getting the machine. I didn't leave a message because," he faltered, rubbing his forehead, "I kept thinking Charlie'd come through the door and I'd have to apologize for getting hysterical. I don't know. I hate those things."

"Maybe they're together." It calmed me to consider this. Carmen was a good kid. So was Charlie, but she could be erratic, emotional. Hot-headed. Carmen reined her in.

"Maybe."

I took advantage of this moment of semi-calm. "Why don't you go home and order us a pizza? I'll stop by Carmen's house on my way."

He hesitated, seeming as unsure as I was of my leadership.

I stood up as if it was decided. "We'll figure out the next step over dinner. And, hey, maybe she'll be home when you get back."

He got to his feet and we headed to our cars. As he was getting in his SUV, I shouted: "If she's there, call me right away."

He nodded, climbed inside, and drove off.

Carmen lived in one of those developments with three different housing plans repeated a few dozen times and painted in HOA approved pastels. It would be easy to get lost if I didn't know the neighborhood by heart, having spent all the years since I got my license picking up or dropping off. I took the corner onto her street and was awash with relief: there, in the stubby driveway, was Charlie's yellow Volkswagen bug.

By the time I rang the doorbell, my relief had already turned to anger. What was she thinking? How could she let us worry like that – especially my poor father. He'd missed a day at work, something he never did, indicative of just how scared he'd been.

I banged on the door, righteous adrenaline behind every thud.

It was Carmen who came to the door. I could just make her out through the mesh of the security screen: dark hair flat on one side, wild on the other. She was wearing a red tank top and baggy shorts that hung low on her tiny hips.

"Olivia." She gasped my name in a gravelly voice and reached to unlock the security door. As I pulled it open, her face crumpled and she stepped back. "Oh, god."

It was not the welcome I'd expected. I tried to hold my voice steady. "Where's Charlie?"

Carmen blinked and her face smoothed. "You don't know?"

"No, I don't know!" I was yelling. Suddenly, I felt like I wanted to hit her, this girl I'd known forever who was nearly as much a sister as Charlie was. She knew something; she was hiding something, taunting me.

Carmen put a hand to her chest. "Oh, you scared me. I thought you were coming to tell me something had happened."

"Something like what?"

"I don't know. I've been texting her all day and she hasn't texted back. I'm worried."

"Her car's in your driveway."

"I know. She was here last night." And then, finally: "Come in." She shut the door behind me and led me into the living room.

"My dad was calling the house all day," I said.

She sat in the oversized recliner in the corner and pulled her feet under her, making herself even smaller than she already was. "My parents are away. I don't answer the house phone. It's never for me."

I sat down on the couch across from her. "Carmen, if you were worried about her, why didn't you try to get a hold of me or my dad?"

She looked startled by this suggestion. "I didn't want to get her in trouble."

I sighed. *Kids*. "So she was here last night?"

Carmen nodded, warily.

"Did she sleep here?"

"Well, I thought she did. But, I'm not sure."

"When was the last time you saw her?"

"I went to bed at about one and she was still up."

"What was she doing?"

"Well, there were some other people here. And they were all just talking."

"And you went to bed while a bunch of people were in your house?"

"Not a bunch. A couple. And I was tired."

"Drunk?"

She stammered and I rolled my eyes. "Carmen. I don't care. I just want to find my sister. Who else was here?"

"When I went to bed, it was just Charlie and Isaac."

"I thought you said there were a couple people."

She shrugged.

"Who's Isaac?"

"Um, I don't know his last name. He's in Charlie's ethics class. They're kind of a thing."

"Charlie has a boyfriend?"

"It's new," Carmen said quickly, trying to cushion the blow.

What else didn't I know? I was the cool older sister Charlie idolized and confided in. I'd been the one to take her to Planned Parenthood when things started getting serious with her high school boyfriend. I kept her secrets from our father and offered wisdom without judgment. What had happened?

"And everyone was gone when you got up this morning?"

"Well, Dan was here. With me."

It was like pulling teeth. Like I cared if her boyfriend slept over. "What time?"

"Around noon. No one was here, but she'd locked up the house from the outside, with her key." Carmen had a key to my dad's house too.

"And no note?"

She shook her head. "And no text and she hasn't been on Facebook."

I looked at my watch. My father would have gotten home by now. No phone call. "This isn't like her." I said it like a statement, but I was looking for reassurance.

"I know." Carmen wrapped her bare arms tightly around herself. "She always texts me back, even in the middle of the night. She keeps her phone with her while she sleeps and she'll just send me back a smiley face so I know she's listening."

Among a group of framed photographs on the surface of a dresser, there was a shot of the two girls with their faces pressed together, grinning. They were both missing their front teeth, which would make them, what, six or seven? Their faces were painted like butterflies, caterpillar middles along the bridge of their noses, antennae on their foreheads. It had been taken at the 4th Avenue Street Fair; there was a copy of that photograph at my dad's house.

I turned back to Carmen. "How well do you know this Isaac?"

"I've only met him a few times, but he seems okay. Kind of quiet."

"Do you know how to get a hold of him?"

She shook her head. "Charlie had his number."

"How drunk was she when you went to bed?"

"Just tipsy. Not out of control. I wouldn't have left if she was trashed."

"I know. But they were still drinking when you left?"

She nodded. "It was just beer. I cleaned up all the empties this morning."

I rubbed my palms against the top of my thighs. They were so clammy. I was worried for nothing, I told myself. She was nineteen and I hadn't heard from her in a day. That was nothing. "If you hear from her, or you think of anything, call me, okay?" I stood up.

Carmen nodded.

Before I left, I tried the door to the bug, but it was locked. I cupped my hands around my eyes and peered through the window. There, sitting in one of the cup holders, was Charlie's cell phone.

"Well, that explains why she hasn't called us," I said. My dad and I were sitting on barstools around the island in the kitchen, the only part of the house that had been renovated. It had followed months of arguments between my parents and an endless stream of bickering while it was being done. My mother had insisted on this island; it was the necessary feature of any respectable kitchen.

"No," my father said. "That explains why she didn't get our messages, not why she hasn't called. No excuse."

He'd already called to update the police on this and the location of the car. They'd added these details to the report he filed earlier, but sounded generally unimpressed. It's not against the law for an adult to go missing. That's what they'd told him. When he repeated it to me, he had a sneer on his face and a mocking tone in his voice.

"If she still had her phone, we could track her with the GPS," he said with his mouth full.

"I never thought of that."

"The detective told me." He sighed. "She could be anywhere."

My pizza cooled on the plate in front of me. "There's got to be an explanation. She doesn't have her phone so she doesn't have our numbers?"

My dad looked at me without any facial expression at all, but somehow managed to convey his belief in my absurdity. It was a stretch. My father's home number had been the same our entire lives.

I tried again. "She isn't near a phone."

"Where could she be that isn't near a phone?"

"Maybe she and Isaac got separated. Maybe his car broke down. Maybe she's lost in the desert somewhere."

"Do you know how cold it gets at night?"

"Cold. But not hypothermia cold."

He got to his feet quickly, just catching his stool before it tipped over.

"Where are you going?"

"It gets colder in the mountains."

"So, what, you're going to drive up Mt Lemmon?"

"I guess. I can check out the camping areas." He ran his hand over his head, attempting to smooth his hair but only succeeding in making himself look more agitated.

"You're just going to drive around all night?"

"Do you have any better ideas?"

"Can I come?"

"No. You stay here. Call me if she comes home."

My father's frantic day was spelled out in the living room: photo albums spread across the coffee table, his laptop on the couch, a list of hospital contact information on the screen.

My father had resisted the shift to digital; he loved getting his prints in the mail, pressing them under the cellophane pages. He held out much longer than the majority of Luddites; the most recent album was from Charlie's high school graduation. Her hair was long then, darker than my own mousy brown, which I'd lightened for so long that my natural color could only be found in these albums, the early ones.

Charlie looked so sweet in these photos. This was before the nose ring, before the Virgin Mary tattoo on her left forearm, before she chopped her hair short and sculpted it into a fine point along the center of her skull. That happened the following summer, her transformation for college into somebody cool, somebody tough. But she hadn't changed her personality: a little shy, soft spoken. It made the external changes seem incongruous.

Though really, Charlie had always been a bit of a contradiction. She was so uncomfortable as the center of attention and yet very prone to melodrama. It made for an interesting adolescence. She did not tantrum in public. But she'd fix you with a cold stare and you'd know you were in for it later. She could make you miserable by withholding her usual charm, substituting a dedicated sulk my father referred to as her death look. She had a commitment to the silent treatment that I couldn't help but be in awe of.

I sat on the couch and reached for one of the photo albums at the bottom of the pile. It was one of the older ones, the adhesive yellowed with age. There was Charlie as a newborn, a pink, hospital-issue cap hiding her mass of black hair. My mother sat in a hospital bed, looking tired but so happy it made me queasy. How could that have been real? Somehow, it would have made more sense if she weren't holding Charlotte so tight, if her eyes in these pages were not focused on the photographer (my dad) or on her children, but instead looking distractedly, longingly, out the window. But, they were not.

I'd looked for answers in these pages before, knew there were none to be found. These were the good days, the days we'd posed for the camera, the days we wanted to remember forever.

And yet, for me at least, the crisper memories were of the other days, the ones not in photographs. I could still hear her screaming in Spanish, throwing plates at my father. Charlotte didn't remember these things, didn't remember how I shut her in my bedroom and turned up the stereo. For her, these photos had become the real memories. For me, they were an elaborate and convincing charade.

Toward one in the morning, I went to Charlie's room to find something to sleep in. I was distracted though, rifling through her drawers. Sitting on the floor, I turned the pages of several half-filled notebooks. Charlie was not an organized student; the same notebook was used for several classes and the subjects weren't segregated. This one held philosophy notes and biology notes and shopping lists. Several pages that began with a definition of terms devolved into swirly doodles. In separate locations, I found three phone numbers without identifying names.

I set these aside and reached for her high school yearbook. The only photo of Charlie in this book was her senior photo, the little square that preceded a list of memories that read like gibberish. So many abbreviations, I doubted even she would remember what they referred to in a few years' time.

My face could be found all through my high school yearbook. I'd been on teams: field hockey, basketball, softball. I'd been on the yearbook staff as well, which meant I was in the candids section, along with all my friends.

I hardly spoke to any of them any more, the ones who stayed in town. I'd been popular in high school but I envied the intimate bond Charlie had with Carmen. They didn't join teams or go to parties, but they had each other. In all my years of high school, I'd never really trusted any of those girls who were my friends. I'd seen too many casualties of the clique, girls who committed some random faux pas and found themselves on the outs. I used to tell people my mother had died and I never mentioned that she was Mexican. My dad was white; I had a white last name. And my brown little sister was little enough not to be around too often.

At 4 AM, I collapsed fully dressed into my old bed across the hall.

2. Wednesday

In the morning, I found my father in the kitchen, sitting at the island. Against the far wall, the kitchen table sat empty, covered in several layers of clutter. My father was dressed for work like maybe things were back to normal. But he wasn't reading the paper like normal. He was writing on a yellow legal pad. I stood over his shoulder and tried to make sense of his scribbles.

"So, I guess you didn't find her." I got a mug from the cabinet and poured myself the rest of the coffee.

He didn't answer, just forcefully underlined something in his notes. Twice.

"Are you going in to work?" My father ran his own dental practice and yesterday had been the first day he'd taken off in as long as I could remember.

He shook his head. "I need you to drive me to Carmen's. So I can pick up Charlie's car." He wasn't asking. "Do you know her passwords? For her cell phone or her email?"

I sat down. "No."

He looked up at me then, as if to check for dishonesty in my face.

"I really don't. I could try talking to Carmen again." It seemed like she was the true keeper of secrets these days.

He nodded. "I'd talk to Carmen myself, but you'd probably get more out of her on your own."

I agreed. My dad was pretty gruff and came off as intimidating even when he didn't mean to. He was liable to make Carmen cry.

He cleared his throat and continued looking at his notes on the table. "You'd tell me if you thought she could be . . . pregnant. Or something."

I blinked, startled by his bluntness. "I'm sure it's nothing like that."

He grunted into his coffee mug.

I'd gotten my first period at thirteen, mere months after my mother had left us. Remembering the conversation I'd had to have with my father still made me squirm with discomfort. I wasn't sure which one of us had been more miserable. He'd gone to Walgreens and came back with a dozen different brands and styles of feminine products, like he'd just swiped a random armload into his cart and run from the aisle. In the years that followed, whenever we went to the grocery store, he'd hand over the cart at the end of the trip and let me go get whatever "personal items" I needed.

When Charlie got her period, she'd had me.

My father stood and carried his empty mug to the sink where he could talk with his back to me. "She's been kind of sullen the last couple days."

"Sullen?"

"Quieter than usual. She stayed in her room most of the time she was home. She ate her dinner in there Sunday night."

"Was that unusual?"

He turned and slouched against the counter with his arms folded. I noticed the salt and pepper of his hair was getting saltier. "We usually eat together on Sunday night. But she made herself a frozen pizza. Said she had to study." He shrugged. "I didn't really think anything of it at the time."

"And why would you?" He was wracking his brain to find a clue, but that wasn't anything. Maybe she had been studying or maybe she'd had a fight with this new boyfriend. There was no way to know and it didn't explain her disappearance either way.

The typical reasons young girls ran away – the unplanned pregnancy, the drugs – just didn't apply to Charlie. For any of those things, she'd come to me for help. I was sure of it. I simply couldn't imagine a problem so big she wouldn't reach out. Perhaps my imagination was failing.

"Are you ready?" he asked, straightening up.

I looked into the still full cup of coffee in front of me. "Sure."

My father and I stood in front of the Rodriguez house as I tried to guess the password on Charlie's phone.

I shook my head.

My dad sighed and turned away without saying a word. He backed Charlie's car out of the driveway while I banged away on the front door. It was early and it took Carmen a good ten minutes to figure out I wasn't a Jehovah's Witness and I wasn't going away.

"Olivia," she grumbled sleepily, letting me in.

"When do your parents get back?"

"Tomorrow."

I followed her into the kitchen where she yanked open the refrigerator and gazed inside, groggily. "Do you want anything?"

"No thanks."

She settled on some orange juice, poured herself a glass and sat next to me at the breakfast bar.

"Has she called you?" I asked.

Carmen shook her head.

"Would you tell me if she had?"

She hesitated. "I guess it depends."

"On?"

"On whether she asked me to keep it a secret."

I rolled my eyes.

"Well?" She shrugged. "She's my best friend."

"I know, but—" I shook my head. "Something's wrong. You know it."

Carmen wouldn't look at me, feigning fascination with the fraying hem of her t-shirt.

"My father's worried sick." It pissed me off how tranquil she seemed. I wanted to shake her. "He's afraid she could be dead!"

She cringed. "She hasn't called me, Olivia, I swear. I'm as worried as you are."

Whenever Carmen and Charlie got into trouble as girls, Carmen was the first to cave in. She was not a confident liar, unlike my sister, who could commit to the most outrageous fictions. Carmen tapped her ragged fingernails against the still-full glass of orange juice. I tended to believe her.

"Do you know any of her passwords?" I asked.

Her eyes bulged. "Even if I did." She looked away and shook her head.

It drove me nuts, but I couldn't really blame her. "Are there other things going on in Charlie's life that I don't know about?"

"Olivia," she whined. She scratched at her bare thigh. She was so skinny. "I'm not just going to tell you all her secrets."

Secrets.

I sighed heavily. Carmen had been the last person I knew to lay eyes on my baby sister. 1 AM on Tuesday. It was only Wednesday morning, I reminded myself, but for some reason it didn't comfort me. "If she contacts you, will you tell her to call me?"

"Yes. But I can't make her. I mean, to be honest, if she calls me, I'll probably do whatever she tells me to do."

"I know." I reached into my bag, wrote my number on the back of an old grocery list. "But my dad's frantic. If you hear from her please just let us know she's okay." I stood up and pressed the folded paper into her hand. Of course she already had my number, but now she couldn't pretend otherwise.

I was already late for work by the time I parked in front of my apartment, but it couldn't be helped. I had to change my clothes, but more than that, I had to feed Oscar.

I had my key in the lock when I heard a voice behind me.

"Walk of shame?"

I jumped a bit and turned to see Rick leaning on the hood of my car. "What? No!" Not that it was any of his business. "I slept at my dad's." I turned back to the door and shoved it open. It was getting too hot for outdoor conversations.

Rick followed me inside without being asked. He was wearing a bright blue, billowy dress shirt that looked too big for him. It was visual proof of our break up; he'd started dressing himself. Luckily, no one in the IT department where he worked was likely to notice. At the office parties I'd gone to, most of his coworkers had worn t-shirts with cartoon characters on them.

I pulled my bag off over my head and tossed it on the kitchen table with my keys. Oscar was already sitting in the corner beside his empty food dish, glaring at me.

I sing-songed apologies to the cat. I let him eat directly from the can.

"Is your dad okay?" Rick asked, sitting at my table.

"Yes." I shook my head "No. He's worried about Charlie. She hasn't been home for two nights."

"Charlie?" He sounded appropriately surprised.

"Yeah. It's bad, right? I mean, something must be really wrong."

"Bad?" He tipped his chair back, contemplating. "Nah. I'm sure she's fine. Just getting up to some age-appropriate shenanigans."

Rick had known Charlie since she was fifteen. "She's never done anything like this before," I said, slowly, trying to keep the irritation out of my voice. This should not have been news to him.

He waved his arm dismissively. "Don't you remember what it felt like to be nineteen?"

I considered this. When I was nineteen, I was a full time college student with a part time job answering phones at my dad's office. I'd had a thirteen year old to take care of.

"I guess my nineteen was different from yours," I said, folding my arms across my chest.

Rick sighed heavily. "Right." He sounded almost sarcastic. "Well, maybe your nineteen was different from Charlie's, too."

"Maybe." I just wanted him to stop tipping in the chair. The last thing I needed was Rick splitting his head open on my floor.

"You worry too much," he said. "So serious."

"Why are you here, anyway?"

"Just checking in."

I frowned.

"When I drove by last night, your car was gone. I just wanted to be sure you were okay."

"Well, that's . . ." I swallowed the word *creepy*. "Not your job."

Rick shrugged. "Old habits."

I sighed. Rick was a good guy. We'd met my senior year of college at a party thrown by a friend of mine whose name I no longer remembered. I hadn't realized at the time that it was a set up, that we'd been left alone together in the back yard on purpose. He was chatty, which I loved. Listening is good too, but growing up with the strong, silent type as a father made me appreciate a man who could hold up his end of a conversation. Conversations were my favorite.

"Maybe you're the one who worries too much." I raked my fingers through my hair.

"Maybe so."

It seemed so long ago. I felt like a totally different person now, but here he was, sitting in my kitchen: the same confident, chatty boy I'd met all those years ago. "I'm late for work," I said and left him at the table while I went to change.

On my lunch break, I sat in the courtyard with a soda and a small bag of chips. It was as private as you could get in April, when everyone took shelter indoors. I always had to bring a sweater to work – even in July. The warmer it got outside, the colder people liked their air conditioning.

I thought it was a bit much. Growing up, we'd always used a swamp cooler, which worked just fine until the monsoon. The cooler couldn't do much for about a month when it got really humid. In the summers, it was my job to watch Charlie while our dad was at work. It would get too hot for bike riding and there were only so many people in our neighborhood with pools. We spent most afternoons lying in front of the television on the cool Saltillo tile, watching telenovelas we only half understood. So much could be conveyed through hand gestures and the tone of voice, our rudimentary Spanish filled in the rest. At the commercial, we'd roll to a cooler spot on the tile.

Now, I pictured her body crumpled at the base of a jagged cliff, her bones picked clean in the desert, or battered and rotting in a shallow grave. I held my head in both my hands and let out three short sobs.

"Are you okay?"

I looked up, wiping my cheeks with my palms. I'd thought I was alone, but there was a man sitting behind a row of plants where there were no seats. He came rolling toward me now, in a wheelchair, looking concerned.

"I'm fine, I'm fine." I tried to laugh.

His thick, dark brows careened together.

"Really. I'm fine. I—" I sighed. "I didn't know anyone was out here." The first true thing.

"Yeah. Sorry about that. You know, if it seemed like I was hiding back there. I didn't mean to."

"It's okay." I shrugged, pushed my hair back and thought for a moment. "Please don't tell anyone you saw me out here crying. It would be—" What was the word? "Embarrassing."

"Don't worry. I wouldn't do that. I'm not sure I'm going in there anyway."

"First day?"

"Yep."

"It's not so bad."

"No?"

"Well, I guess I've never been on your end of it. So it's not really fair for me to say."

"You're one of the physical therapists?"

I nodded. "I could even be yours. What's your name?"

"Greg. But I think I've got a guy."

"Mmm. Probably Phil. He's really nice. And funny. You should give him a shot." His face was noncommittal.

When I thought about the rest of my day's appointments, the only man's name I could remember was Mr. Lopez. He'd had a hip replacement three weeks ago and was already on his last appointment covered by insurance. I was worried he wouldn't keep up his exercises after he left. Hopefully, I could give my goodbye talk in front of his wife.

"I'm Olivia," I said, because it felt weird for me to know his name if he didn't know mine.

"Hi, Olivia. So now that you know why I was hiding, you want to tell me why you were crying?"

"I thought you said you weren't hiding."

He grinned. He was really handsome when he let his face do that.

I took a deep breath and spoke on the exhale. "My sister's missing." I hadn't really been telling anyone, hadn't said it out loud in quite those terms. "My little sister." My voice broke and I had to swallow the brick in my throat.

"Oh, no. That's awful. I'm so sorry." His eyebrows were crashing together again.

"Thank you."

"How long has she been missing?"

"A little over twenty-four hours." I forced a laugh. "That might not seem like a long time, but if you knew her." I shrugged. "It's a long time."

"How old is she?"

"Nineteen."

He shook his head, seemed to swallow a few more questions he thought better of. "I have a little sister about that age. I can't imagine how that must be for you."

It felt good to have validation, even from a stranger.

I glanced at my watch. "I gotta get to my next appointment." I narrowed my eyes at him. "You should get going too."

"I took the bus so I'm still early. I have another whole hour to chicken out."

I stood up. "Well, don't. Phil's cool. You'll like him."

He nodded, still making no promises, and I let myself back into the refrigerated building.

At the end of the day, I sat at a table in the empty break room and checked my voicemail. There was Carmen's little voice telling me she'd tracked down Isaac's last name and he'd been on Facebook. I listened to the rest of the message as I jogged to my car. I called her back as I started the engine and turned up the AC.

"What did he say?" I tilted my head, sandwiching the phone between my ear and shoulder as I eased out of the parking space. I used to make Charlie pull off the road whenever she answered my phone call from her car. It was a condition of my dad paying her insurance and she never complained.

"It's his status update. It says: 'Charlie happened in Vegas so she's staying there! Hashtag, girlsarecrazy.'"

"What the hell does that mean?"

"I don't know. Like: 'what happens in Vegas stays in Vegas'?"

"So they went to Las Vegas?" I turned onto the main road.

"I guess."

"And he left her there?"

"That's what it sounds like to me."

"So she's stranded in Vegas. Fine. But why wouldn't she call?" My dad might think it was irresponsible of her to take off in the middle of the week, missing classes to go off with some boy, but it wasn't as if there was much he could do about it. He certainly wasn't going to kick her out over it. It was not knowing she was okay that would make him irate. And beyond that, it was just so unkind to make him worry, make all of us worry, if there was truly nothing to worry about. I couldn't imagine why she'd put us through this.

"Carmen, was Charlie mad at us?"

"What do you mean?"

"I keep trying to make it make sense. Are you positive she didn't leave a note behind?"

"Yeah. Totally."

I gripped the steering wheel tighter. It made no sense.

"Do you want me to send Isaac a message?" Carmen asked.

"No. I need to talk to him face to face. How can I find him?"

"His last name is Paulson. I could maybe find his address if I cyber stalk him. Or you could find him on campus. I think Charlie's got Ethics tomorrow. You could catch him outside before class. Assuming he goes. It's at 8AM."

"Email me his picture." I stopped at a light. "Don't message him. I don't want him to have time to think up a story."

"You think he might have hurt her?"

"Do you?"

"I don't know! I don't think so, but, oh my *god*." Her voice cracked and in the silence that followed, I thought she was crying.

The light turned green and I was lost in a horrible fantasy. My sister being brutalized in a hotel room. Drugged, robbed, beaten, humiliated. Unfortunately, there were so many ways young women could be hurt by young men who seemed harmless. "There's got to be some explanation." I heard myself reassuring her. "I just don't understand why she wouldn't call. One of us."

I hung up to the sound of Carmen sniffling. I had to fight the urge to join in. What the fuck was Charlie doing in Las Vegas?

That night, I decided to make meatloaf. Not knowing what my father would have in the kitchen, I stopped at the store for supplies. I picked up a blue plastic basket at the front of the store and became absorbed in the task at hand. For the next fifteen or twenty minutes, my mind focused on the list. Hamburger, eggs, breadcrumbs. Surely they had ketchup.

It wasn't until after they scanned my items, after I'd swiped my card, after the cashier had wished me the requisite good evening that I sat in my car and remembered why I wasn't going back to my apartment.

"So he just left her in Las Vegas?" My father stood over me as I cracked eggs into a metal bowl. I always started with the eggs. It saved me having to pick eggshell out of the meat.

"Supposedly." Before I'd moved out, I made dinner five nights a week. The three of us sat down at the round table in the kitchen. Since I'd left, they'd stocked up on frozen dinners. The kitchen table was covered in papers, an empty pizza box and a sweatshirt.

"Without a phone?"

"Looks like."

"Where does he live? I'll go talk to him right now."

"I couldn't find his address. He probably lives with his parents. A lot of Paulsons in Tucson." I pushed my fingers into the meaty mixture. This was my favorite part.

"I bet that detective could track him down."

"Maybe. But even if he could, getting the police involved might just scare the kid. I want to get him to talk."

"Fine, but I'm going with you tomorrow. He'll talk if he knows what's good for him. I'll knock some sense into that little punk."

"I don't think that's a good idea." I went to the sink and turned on the faucet with my elbow.

"Why not? No offense, Olivia, but you're not a very intimidating figure."

I laughed. "I'm not interested in roughing him up, Dad. He's a kid." I pulled the meatloaf pan out of a high cabinet and set it next to the bowl.

"What if he hurt your sister?" He said it quietly, as if there was someone else in the house who might overhear.

My arms were covered in goose flesh and I looked into his eyes. "If he hurt her, I'll kill him." I paused to steady my breathing. "But I'm sure he didn't. They're teenagers. They had a stupid fight."

"And he just left her there?" He began pacing the kitchen like a caged lion. "I should just get in the car now. I could be there by morning."

"And then what? How are you going to find one little girl in the middle of Las Vegas? Besides, she could be on her way back. There are buses." I'd checked. For less than a hundred dollars, she could catch the bus at CircusCircus or Treasure Island or Excalibur. It would get to Tucson at two-thirty in the morning. It occurred to me that I could meet it at the station. If I'd been left in Vegas without a cell phone, that's what I would do. Well, I'd find a way to call first, but then I'd take the bus.

Assuming she had her credit card. Did payphones even exist anymore? Would she ask to borrow a stranger's cell phone? She'd always hated talking to strangers.

The oven beeped and I slid the pan onto the rack.

3. Thursday

At 2AM, I watched twenty-seven people, none of whom were my sister, get off the bus from Las Vegas. There was one girl in a hoodie who made me look twice. I leaned against my steering wheel and squinted into the dusk, but as she crossed the street to her ride, she let the hood fall. Her hair was blond.

I went back to my apartment and tried to sleep, but I was so worried I'd miss my alarm that I watched the clock all night. I got up before the alarm even went off. I'd had time for a long shower and to sit in the drive-thru line at Starbucks. I'd made it to Pima Community College by 7:30.

I perked up whenever a black car drove in the lot. All Carmen could tell me was that Isaac drove something "black and sporty." I didn't really know anything about cars myself. To me, that meant everything from a Corvette to a Taurus.

I'd printed off the photo of Isaac that Carmen sent. It was a little square in the top left corner of the paper. I had it spread over the steering wheel and my eyes darted from the page to the world outside my window.

I trusted Carmen when she said she hadn't heard from Charlie. It would have been much more reassuring if I thought she knew more than me. That Charlie hadn't even confided in her was so unsettling.

Charlie was in her second year at Pima. When she'd graduated high school, she'd had no idea what she wanted to study. We all decided it made the most sense for her to figure it out at community college prices, get some of her basic requirements out of the way, and transfer to a more prestigious university when she was a junior. It seemed like a good plan. But in the last two years, Charlie had changed her mind so drastically that none of her courses even counted toward the same major. Creative writing, graphic design, accounting. This semester she was taking animal anatomy and clinical pathology and pharmacology; she'd decided to be a vet tech.

I'd gone to the University of Arizona and lived at home until my last year of school, when I felt I'd finally earned the right to my own life. Charlie graduated from high school and I moved into my own apartment the following July. A year later, I finished my degree and accepted the position at Desert Oasis. I'd been working there for nearly a year.

The day I moved out, Charlie helped by unpacking the boxes I hauled across town. She put away silverware and made my bed and affixed the phone numbers for all the local delivery restaurants to my refrigerator, under a photo magnet of the two of us posed by the otter exhibit at the Desert Museum. At the end of the night, instead of driving her home, I drove up Mt. Lemmon, stopping at one of our favorite pull outs. It was about twenty degrees cooler up there, looking over the edge of the cliff at the city lights or up at the stars. We sat on the hood of the car with our drive-thru sodas.

We were talking about something like getting curtains for my kitchen when she started crying. Begrudgingly, I put my arm around her. I couldn't help feeling a little resentful that she couldn't just be happy for me. She had to make it all about her. It had always been this way.

"I'm not even that far away," I reminded her.

"But it's not the same," she whimpered.

"Of course it's not the same," I said. "That's life."

It turned out Isaac drove a Firebird. When I saw him, there was no mistaking it. He had dark hair and a narrow face, a long nose, dark eyes and lashes. He was good looking, but a bit too thin. He wore black skinny jeans and a messenger bag hanging low on one shoulder, looking as if it might tip him over.

I stepped out of the car and it seemed like the slam of my car door was the only sound in the lot. He'd parked further away and would have to pass me to get to the building. I stepped in front of him when he was still a few strides away. "Isaac," I said. "I need to talk to you."

He slowed, looking uncertain. "I'm on my way to class."

"I know. You're going to be late." And then, because he looked prepared to disagree, I introduced myself: "I'm Olivia Howard. Charlie's my little sister."

He sighed then, like it was all very irritating, and I took some degree of comfort that he did not look particularly guilty as I imagined he would have if he'd recently stuffed my sister's body in a dumpster.

"Look, Charlie's a big girl. If she has a problem with me, she can speak for herself." He shifted his bag to his other shoulder.

"Well, I'm relieved to hear you think so, since no one has heard from her in days."

"You mean she's not back?"

"No, she's not. She hasn't been home since Monday morning and no one has heard from her. Not even Carmen."

He pushed his hand through his hair and shifted his weight. "Well, she lost her cell phone, but that's all I can tell you. I really gotta get to class."

He started walking past me, but I grabbed his wrist. I remembered my father saying I wasn't physically intimidating enough and realized he never would have said that if he'd seen this willowy little boy. My half-hearted grip on his wrist was more than enough to prevent his forward motion.

"You need to talk to me," I said. "My dad's about to give your name to the police."

"The police?"

"As far as we know, you were the last person to see or hear from her. We're all pretty worried."

I motioned to an empty picnic table at the edge of the parking lot and he followed me, his shoulders slumped like he was on his way to the principal's office.

As he took the seat across from me, he was already beginning his excuses. "Just so you know, I offered her my cell phone, but she kept saying it was better to ask for forgiveness instead of permission."

I nodded. "And where was this?"

"Las Vegas."

"Whose idea was that?"

"I don't know. It was kind of mutual. We were talking about it and she said she'd never been. I said we should go sometime. And then 'sometime' became right then. It was just a natural progression to the conversation. It was organic."

"Hm." *Organic*. I didn't have time to make fun of the way he talked. "Okay. When did you get there?"

"Tuesday morning. When we got to the hotel, we just went to sleep. We'd been driving all night."

"What hotel?"

"The Flamingo."

"And what did you do there? After you woke up?"

"Well, I got up first and I played some Blackjack. When Charlie found me, she was mad I hadn't woken her up. Then she got over it and we went to a bar."

"Charlie's only nineteen"

"She has a fake I.D."

I tried not to let on that this surprised me. I knew Charlie drank, but I pictured the kind of underage drinking that I'd done, in basements and friend's houses, relying on someone's parents to go away, someone's older brother to buy the booze. A fake I.D. suggested a deeper level of rebellion.

"Okay. What else did you do?"

He shrugged "It's Vegas. We gambled, we drank, we went back to the hotel room."

If at all possible, I didn't want to know what they did in the hotel room.

"And then you left her there?" I said.

"We fought again Wednesday morning. Yesterday."

"About?"

"She got really opinionated about me gambling. I don't know. It was messed up. I told her to get off my back and it didn't go over well."

I could imagine.

"So she stormed off. I told her I was leaving at *noon*." He emphasized this by pressing his index finger against the tabletop. "I didn't want to get charged for another night so I went back to the room to get our stuff and check out. Her backpack was there, but not her. And she didn't have her phone so I couldn't call her!" He threw his hands up with an exasperation he seemed to think I'd have sympathy for. "I didn't know what to do so I left her bag at the front desk. They said they'd give it back to her if she showed up."

"And then you left her there."

"What was I supposed to do?"

I leaned across the table. "Not leave her there. Not leave a young woman without a cell phone or a car several hours away from anyone she knows in the middle of Las Vegas."

"Look, I said I was sorry."

I replayed our conversation in my head. "Actually, you didn't."

"Well, I'm sorry! Okay? I don't know why she isn't back yet. I just figured she'd take a bus. I'm sure she's fine."

My right hand was gripping the outer edge of the table and I was shaking. "You better hope she's fine."

"Whatever." He stood up and stepped over the bench. "I'm going to class. I told you everything I know."

I watched him walk away.

The waiting room at my father's office was empty.

Mrs. Carver had been my father's receptionist since he opened the practice. She was short and sturdy with long white hair and bright blue eyes. She wore black mascara and streaks of rouge that created the illusion of cheekbones. Her lipstick came off on her morning coffee cup and she spent the day with her pale mouth outlined in pink.

"Olivia!" She rushed out from behind her desk as soon as I came in.

"Hey, Mrs. Carver," I said as she hugged me. She gave the best hugs, warm and bosomy and smelling of Chantilly. I'd never called her by her first name even when I'd worked here.

"Your father," she said, shaking her head. "I told him not to come in, but there was an emergency. Jim Taylor broke a crown."

She led me down the hall to his office. "He should be done soon, dear. Can you tell me anything about our girl?"

Mrs. Carver had taken care of Charlie from the time she was born. My dad used to bring her to the office to give my mother a break. No one could complain since he was the boss. Besides, I never got the impression that Mrs. Carver was faking her affection. She had grandchildren who lived across the country and we benefited from her loss. Later, when my mom was gone, Charlie would take the bus here after school whenever I had practice. She did her homework at my father's desk. She'd practically grown up in this office. We both had. She'd started working here when she was sixteen.

"I'm still not really sure. It looks like she got stranded in Las Vegas, but I can't figure out why she wouldn't call." I took off my bag and hung it over the back of the chair in front of my father's wide desk.

"You talked to this boyfriend?"

I nodded. My dad must have filled her in.

"Did you believe him?"

I took the chair, shifting it first so I could face Mrs. Carver as she stood in the doorway. "I guess so. I mean, he's a jerk but a believable jerk."

She smiled. "Well, I'm praying for her."

"Thank you."

"Can I get you a coffee or something? Water?"

"No, I'm fine."

"Okay, then. I better get back."

I nodded.

My father's office consisted of three walls of built-in bookcases and one wall behind his desk with a framed print of calla lilies by Diego Rivera. Charlie had given it to him for father's day years ago. It was much more her taste than his, but he hung it up loyally.

My father started his own practice when I was very young. He'd been my dentist my whole life and I'd only ever had one cavity. I'm not sure which one of us was more ashamed.

Charlie liked to brag that she'd never had a cavity. I still remembered the way the Novocain made half my face feel so numb that I kept touching my jaw to be sure it was still there.

My father had a way with older patients, many of whom had been traumatized as children by barbaric practices. This Mr. Taylor was one of those. He refused to let anyone else touch him, not even Nadia, the sweet dental hygienist who'd been working here for a decade.

My dad walked in and immediately removed his white coat. He settled into the broad leather chair behind his desk and sighed heavily. I imagined he was about to break some bad dental news: I needed braces or, perhaps, a root canal.

"So," he said, which was apparently my cue.

"So." I leaned forward, then back. "He didn't tell me anything different than what we figured out already."

"Las Vegas."

"Yep."

"And you believe him?"

"I think so. I mean, he didn't strike me as a criminal."

"Just a shithead?"

"Right."

"So why haven't we heard from her?"

"It makes no sense," I agreed. "But I had an idea."

My dad lifted his eyebrows.

"Can you check her credit card activity?" My dad got Charlie a credit card when she started college. She made the payments, but his name was on the account.

"I already did. There's nothing."

I jolted upright. "Nothing? That girl uses her credit card to buy a pack of gum."

"Nothing since Monday when she got gas. In Tucson."

I leaned back, sighing at the ceiling.

"I could call the police in Las Vegas." He said it uncertainly, like a theory he was testing.

I scowled. "And say what? Your adult daughter has a loser boyfriend. Is that a police matter? I think they have *actual* missing people in Las Vegas."

He threw up his hands. "Well?"

I didn't have an answer to that. We sat together quietly for a long moment.

"I don't know whether to be pissed or worried," my father said finally. "And until I figure it out, I've got work to do here." He swept his arm across the desk. "Mrs. Carver tells me to take the week off, but there's nothing left to do but wait. What would I do at home? I have patients."

I nodded. I'd decided the same thing myself, but it felt wrong for us to go about our lives as if nothing had changed. I felt schizophrenic, my emotional pendulum swinging between frozen panic and furious impatience.

"At least when your mother left, she had the decency to leave a note."

My sharp intake of breath was audible. We didn't talk about my mother. I'd once found that hard. Now I preferred it. "This is nothing like that," I said.

"No?"

"No. Charlie's coming home."

My father pressed the palm of his hand against his forehead and nodded.

I'd been at the house on Sunday morning to do laundry. It was cheaper than a Laundromat and usually gave me a chance to check in.

Charlie was in the kitchen eating a piece of toast with jam. She was wearing a pale yellow sundress and leaned over the sink as crumbs scattered.

"You look nice." I set the laundry bag down in the doorway.

Charlie looked up at me and – am I misremembering? – made a face. It was fleeting. "Church," she said and I dismissed the look as guilt or annoyance at being caught eating. If you ate before church, you couldn't eat any of those dry wafers. Communion. Such a shame.

Her hair was slicked back, the tiny stud in her nose only visible when it caught the light. Her make-up was muted; she looked the part of the innocent Catholic schoolgirl. Tomorrow, the hair would be spiked, the eyes outlined in black – another role. I supposed it was age-appropriate, but I wondered which version was closer to the truth. I wasn't really fond of either.

"You want to get lunch when you get back?" I sat down at one of the tall island bar stools; her high heel sandals were making me feel short.

She crossed to the refrigerator and pulled out a carton of orange juice. She spoke with her back to me as she poured a short glass. "I'm going to brunch with Carmen after," she said, turning, and drank it down in a long gulp.

I wondered if she was going to pretend she hadn't eaten so that she could receive Communion with the others. Was that a sin? Did sins have different rankings or were eating meat on Friday, using birth control and committing murder all the same? Or did none of it matter anyway since you could just confess and be forgiven for anything?

I didn't ask her any of this. She'd say I was being insulting and I probably was. I didn't get any of it. I was an atheist, though even that was half-hearted. The only time I gave it any thought at all was when my little sister was professing to be a believer.

Charlie had been going to church with the Rodriguez family for nearly her whole life. It was weird; I'd been forced to go to mass every Sunday of my early childhood. I could still remember the hard wooden pews and the uncomfortably tight dress shoes I'd had to wear. I'd never fully understood why we stopped going, but I think it had to do with the fact that my father wasn't really Catholic. I'd never missed it.

Charlie spent so many weekends with Carmen that her Catholicism began without much thought into her religious upbringing; it was just about the convenience of tagging along. But eventually, Carmen started taking Catechism class on weekday evenings and Charlie felt left out. I had to attend mass whenever Charlie made one of the Sacraments: her first communion, confession, confirmation. It was strange the way the old customs returned: dipping a finger in the holy water at the arched entryway, crossing yourself before entering the pew, shaking hands with the strangers seated near you part-way through the service. All the other Sundays, I was free to sleep in while my kid sister voluntarily sacrificed her morning to be part of an archaic, repressive, child-abuse ignoring fraternity.

Carmen tapped her horn in the driveway and Charlie reached for the small white clutch on the counter, completing the costume.

"Goodbye!" I yelled as she rushed out, flapping her arm in my direction.

Now I remembered that Sunday, watching my sister slip out the front door, never thinking it could be the last time I ever saw her. I didn't say anything important or tell her I loved her. I just waved my arm like an idiot who can't see into the future.

4. Friday

I hit the alarm three times and didn't have time to eat breakfast. I'd gone to bed certain that Charlie was fine. Maybe she was embarrassed about the fight with Isaac, blowing off steam before returning. Not calling us was a product of her selfishness, the idea she had that she was at the center of her very own universe.

I'd woken up less certain.

I couldn't concentrate at work, passing a patient off to one of the techs and spending almost an hour texting Carmen in the bathroom.

Why isn't she calling???? I typed forcefully into my phone.

I don't know, came Carmen's reply and I wished I could look in her eyes, hear her tone of voice.

I ate a yogurt while writing progress notes through my lunch hour. My last patient of the day canceled, so I decided to leave early.

Greg had parked his wheelchair at the end of a shiny, green bench at the curb. I'd seen him in the office earlier that day. He'd been walking with the assistance of the parallel bars. I'd wondered whether I should nod a hello, but he'd been so focused, he didn't seem to see me.

"Hey," I said. "You're still here. That can't be good."

He looked up at me and held his hand across his brow, squinting through his fingers.

I shuffled left so the sun wasn't right behind me.

"Yeah. I just called." He held up his cell phone in his other hand. "A couple buses overheated or something. So the whole system is backed up."

"Well, can I give you a ride?"

"Oh, no, that's okay. I mean, thanks, but it's fine. They'll be here eventually."

"Are you sure?"

He didn't answer right away. "I've got a book." He shrugged.

"Look, I'd hate to leave you here. The building's gonna close in an hour and then it gets dark and cold. And it feels like the middle of nowhere. I know cuz I've been left waiting for a ride here."

He laughed. "Who would do that?"

"Boyfriend. Ex-boyfriend."

He laughed again. "Hell, yeah, ex-boyfriend!"

I smiled. I hadn't broken up with Rick that night, but I had given him a ration of shit. He was the one always warning me about which neighborhoods to avoid at night, how to check the back seat before getting in my car. I sat on that bench with my cell phone in my lap. Rick's cell went to voice mail and I couldn't call my dad; he'd be too angry. "Seriously, come on. I got nowhere I gotta be."

"Really? Won't you get in trouble?"

I narrowed my eyes at him. "You gonna tell on me?"

"No, Ma'am."

"All right then. This way."

I was parked at the far end of the lot. I thought about asking if he wanted me to push the chair, but I didn't want to offend him. He seemed to keep up pretty well. As we approached my car, I hit the clicker and opened the passenger side door.

"Is there room in your trunk for the chair?" he asked me.

"Yep. It's empty," I said. "You need a hand getting in?"

"Nope." He set the brake and reached for the top edge of the car door with his right hand. With his left hand, he grabbed hold of the handle on the ceiling of the car. He stood, his balance clearly a bit off, focusing. Slowly, he lifted his left foot and set it on the floor inside. Then he swung his body inside, gripping the door with white knuckles. Before he pulled his right leg inside, he leaned out. "Do you know how to fold that thing up?" he asked, gesturing to the chair.

"Oh, yeah. No problem." I tipped the empty chair forward and dragged it backward on its unlocked front casters. I folded it and hoisted it into the trunk easily.

"Where to?" I asked as I slid behind the wheel.

"Just take a right on River," he said as we both buckled our seatbelts. "I really appreciate this."

"Don't worry about it. I'm out early anyway."

He gestured to his phone. "I have to call and let them know I got a ride."

"Go ahead." I concentrated on taking the left out of the parking lot.

When he finished his call, he sank into the seat with an exaggerated sigh. "You have no idea how nice this is. I thought I'd be home for lunch, so I'm starving."

"Oh, God. You haven't eaten lunch? Do you want to stop and pick something up? A drive-thru?"

He turned to look at me. "You wouldn't mind?"

"No! I might get something myself." The prospect of returning to my apartment and rifling through the freezer to find dinner was disheartening. I was too hungry to cook for myself.

We ended up at one of the fast food places I usually avoided so as not to condone the exploitation of low wage workers and corporate abuse of the welfare system. I abandoned my principles a few times a year, a hungry hypocrite. I refused Greg's offer to pay for me, "in exchange for gas". We split the bill and I parked the car under a tree at the back of the lot. In Tucson, shade was coveted, even in the evening. We cracked the windows and undid our seatbelts. I sunk my teeth into my burger and moaned involuntarily.

"It's like crack," Greg agreed.

"Mmmm. For real."

There was a lull as we stuffed ourselves. Then Greg looked up. "Hey. Did you find your sister?"

I swallowed. "Um, not exactly," I said. For some reason I felt embarrassed.

"Oh, wow. Sorry." He stammered, seemed embarrassed too. I wasn't sure if it was for himself, for asking, or for me.

"I sort of tracked her down. Maybe. Her boyfriend says he left her in Las Vegas."

"He left her there?"

"He says they got into an argument and got separated."

"So he just *left* her?"

"That's what he says."

"Ex-boyfriend."

"I hope so." I reached for my soda and fidgeted with the straw, the squeak of plastic on plastic seeming loud against the silence. "She still hasn't called us though, and I don't know if I can believe this little shit."

"Did he tell you which hotel they were staying in?"

"Yeah. The Flamingo. He checked out and left her bag at the front desk."

"Maybe you can call there. Ask if she picked it up."

"I did. They wouldn't give me any information."

"Maybe you should go there. Show her picture? Make a personal appeal."

I mulled that over.

"I'm sorry if I'm overstepping. I don't mean to tell you your business."

"No. I was just thinking that's a good idea. My dad was talking about going the other night, but I stopped him. The thing is, we didn't have anything to go on then. Now we at least have it narrowed down to the hotel." And before, I kept thinking we just had to wait – she'd be in touch or she'd be home – any minute. But there was no reason we hadn't heard from her by now. It had been four days. It might be that the only way to find her was to go to her. Waiting had turned up as much as it was likely to.

"The other thing is that she isn't using her credit card, which is totally odd. Four days in Las Vegas by herself and she doesn't use her credit card?"

"That'd be hard for anyone."

"Right?" I looked up at him. "I'm sorry to unload all of this on you. I just don't know whether to be worried or mad. Like, is she not using her credit card because she got mugged or is she doing it deliberately so we can't find her?"

"Well, if she got mugged you'd expect to see all kinds of fraudulent charges from the muggers."

"Oh yeah. I hadn't thought of that." I looked out the windshield. A tattooed man wearing a wife-beater was crouching to tie the shoe of a tiny girl with dark pigtails. She had an ice cream cone in each hand. There was another reason Charlie might not use her credit card. I wasn't even able to say it out loud: she couldn't. I gathered our empty wrappers and shoved them back into the bag. "Ready?"

Greg nodded and I started the car.

"Anyway, how's physical therapy going? Do you like Phil?"

For the rest of the ride, we stuck to safer topics. Greg had grown up in Ohio. He'd moved here three years ago mostly for the weather. It was so much harder to use a wheelchair in the snow.

Greg lived in an apartment complex called The Palms. I parked beside the handicapped parking space and got his chair out of the back. He rolled up the curb cut, then spun to face me. "I had another thought," he said. "About your sister. Maybe check her internet search history."

I drove straight to my dad's after that. He wasn't home yet so I let myself in and found Charlie's laptop. It turned out she'd Google mapped the drive from Tucson to the Vegas strip so the trip couldn't have been as spontaneous as Isaac said it was.

So much for my judge of character.

There was a diner off route 93 that I remembered from the trip we'd taken when Charlie was little, before my mom left. We'd all had pie.

The first time I'd been to Vegas, I was eleven or twelve. We'd driven the seven hours in our station wagon, listening to the soundtrack to *The Little Mermaid* over and over for Charlie's sake.

The trip followed months of my parents fighting, my mother complaining they never went anywhere or did anything.

Charlie had searched for the Denny's on the strip, which seemed odd. She never ate there. She'd tried and failed several times to be a vegan and was always talking about the evils of factory farming. Ultimately, she decided it was okay to eat a grass-fed, happy cow that hadn't spent its life knee-deep in shit waiting to be a meal. It was the Braveheart theory of cows: every cow has to die sometime; how many cows have truly lived?

The Flamingo Hotel was the last search she'd done.

By the time my father got home, I'd already booked my flight.

"I can come with you."

I shook my head. "I think it's better if someone's here in case she comes back. Which is probably more likely."

Before he could argue, the doorbell rang. He rushed to open it with heartbreaking urgency. As if Charlie would ring the bell.

Mrs. Rodriguez was on the front step. Her husband stood behind her, eyeing the stone walkway at his feet. "Carmen won't get out of the car," Lydia said as my father held the door open for her.

Before they came in, Lydia looked over her shoulder. "We forced her to come but she refuses to get out of the car."

"What's going on?" my father asked.

"She got an email from Charlie. Last night, but she only just told us an hour ago. And, she's actually not sure it really was Charlie." Lydia set her purse on the kitchen counter.

"But it came from Charlie's email account." Jorge added. "We thought you'd want to know."

"Of course." The three of them huddled together at the island. "What did it say?"

It reminded me of the times before when the two girls had gotten in trouble and the three of them had come together to discuss strategy. Once, when they were in junior high, Charlie and Carmen had embarked on a dangerous joint eating disorder. I'd come across a notebook filled with their eating diary, which was really a log of deprivation filled with recipes for liquid cleanses, daily weigh-ins and meal logs. I'd turned the notebook over to my father who immediately phoned the Rodriguez house. The sight of Lydia Rodriguez in my kitchen reassured me that things would be resolved. Lydia was a round woman who spoke quickly, passionately, and with her hands. Her confidence in her words inspired the confidence of others. There was no trouble these young girls could get into that Lydia couldn't get them out of.

I left the grown ups in the kitchen and padded out to the driveway. I opened the car door and slid into the backseat. Carmen's face was puffy and tear-stained.

"Was it her?" I asked.

"I don't know. It was so short."

"What did it say?"

"*I'm okay. I wish I could tell you more. I will explain everything soon.*" Carmen shook her head. "I don't hear anything for days and then all I get is three sentences?"

"Carmen, you know her better than any of us. Is it her?"

"No." She looked up at me. "But if it isn't her, who is it?"

5. Saturday

Rather than continue making lists in my head, I decided to get up and get to it, shooing Oscar out of my suitcase before dumping in my clothes. I didn't bother folding any of it. Jeans, t-shirts, underwear. I didn't own anything that wrinkled. Even my work clothes consisted of things that were stretchy, things with *give*.

I'd spoken to Manny last night about feeding Oscar while I was away. He'd assumed I was going with Rick and I didn't correct him. The explanation was unnecessarily complicated, especially when Rick's truck was still making appearances in the lot overnight.

It probably didn't say good things about the way my life was going that when I went out of town, the only people I notified were my cat-sitter and my father. I'd considered calling Rick, but I couldn't stand the prospect of having another conversation where he told me this was all just the normal behavior of an average nineteen-year-old, as if that's all Charlie was: some generic example for her age bracket.

My father knew where Charlie was every moment of those nineteen years. She called when she was running late, she texted if she decided to stop at Walgreens on her way home. Oh, I wasn't stupid. I knew there were times she claimed to be at Carmen's when she was really somewhere else – otherwise how would she have managed to lose her virginity? But even in those moments, Carmen knew where she was. She was never just nowhere, anywhere.

Charlie had been missing for nearly five days.

I stacked Oscar's canned food on the counter beside the can opener and filled his water bowl. He liked Manny, but he'd still punish me for leaving. The first weekend I'd spent away, I returned to find he'd pooped on my pillow. He hadn't done that again, but I could expect the cold shoulder for a day or two when I got back.

I'd had Oscar for two years. We'd never been allowed pets growing up and once I lived alone, it came to me slowly that I was in charge of myself. Someone at school brought in a cardboard box of homeless kittens. By the end of the day, only the littlest was left. I had the instinct to refuse out of habit – it wasn't allowed. And then I remembered that I decided what was allowed.

When I brought Oscar home, I still hadn't been used to living by myself. I heard every noise, got up in the middle of the night to look out the window or check the locks. That first night, I fell asleep with Oscar curled on my chest, and any noises I heard in the night were easily dismissed as kitten exploration. I slept eight solid hours for the first time since I'd moved out.

I threw in a hairbrush and toothbrush and zipped the suitcase shut. "There's still room if you want to come," I told Oscar as he scowled at me from the doorway. That scowl was what got him his name.

I heard the gravel crunch beneath my dad's tires and I was out the door before he could beep.

"What does that mean: she wishes she could say more? Like, someone won't let her?" My father had one hand on the steering wheel and the other pressed against his forehead and temple.

"I don't know, Dad. Maybe she just didn't want to get into it."

"Into what?"

"I don't *know*." We could go back and forth like this for hours. Days. I didn't know anything more than he did. That's why I had to catch a plane in the first place. "Did you update the detective?"

"I'm afraid he'll take this email as proof that they don't need to look for her."

"They're already not looking for her."

He grunted.

He dropped me at the curb. Since 9/11, there was no way to go inside the airport to see people off. He got out of the car and handed me my little suitcase.

"Try not to worry." It was a stupid thing to say, but I was at a loss, grasping for normalcy. Today he seemed frantic enough to have a heart attack or an aneurysm or to drive off the road. "I'll call you as soon as I know anything."

"Call me when you land," he corrected and he hugged me quickly, kissing the top of my head like he had when I was a kid.

The flight was seat-yourself so I took a spot toward the front, near the window. I felt sorry for individual travelers stuck in the middle seat, sandwiched between strangers. If they looked left or right they could be drawn into a silly conversation with a random old lady. I kept my gaze safely out the window at the bustling activity on the tarmac, the shape of the clouds drifting slowly in the sky.

It was a short flight, two hours. Hardly enough time to fit in the drink cart between take off and landing. I got a Coke. I didn't let myself buy soda for the apartment, but I ordered it whenever I had a chance.

As the plane took me further from home, it became less and less possible to pretend this wasn't any big thing. Even if it had started as a lark, a simple yet uncharacteristic adventure, it had gone on too long. I cursed my overactive imagination, the article I'd read recently about young women kidnapped into the sex trade, the fact that we lived in a world that was so dangerous for our little sisters.

I dug my cell phone out of my bag. The most recent picture I had of Charlie was from Christmas. She was sitting on the blue couch at my dad's with wrapping paper strewn across her lap. She held up a pair of striped legwarmers and beamed an exaggerated, *just what I always wanted* smile. Her short hair was spiky without the gel and her face was free of the garish eyeliner. She looked like herself, like the silly, sweet girl I'd grown up with. I couldn't imagine my life without her.

This was the wrong picture to show people. It wasn't how she'd look in public, in Vegas. I scrolled to find another. There she was, holding Oscar. I couldn't remember when I'd taken it. She often dropped by after one of her evening classes. Lately, she'd taken to asking questions about Oscar's fluid intake, his bowels. He suffered through her attention as she pried his mouth open to look at his gums.

This was more like what she looked like to outsiders. The stiff, pointy hair, the eyeliner, a long sleeved shirt with a hole, inexplicably, for her thumb. I could only really see her when I looked deeper. But who else knew to look deeper?

I shook my head. They existed in every era, slight variations on a stupidly similar theme. Hipsters, emo, goth, punks and hippies. Generations of young people asserting their nonconformity by wearing the exact same thing.

The woman at the front desk of the Flamingo had long glossy blond hair and perfect teeth. I got in her line on purpose. She looked like someone who had sisters. I smoothed the print-out of my reservation on the counter as she typed my information into her computer, passed me my key card and hoped I'd enjoy my stay.

"Were you working on Tuesday? Or Wednesday?"

She looked up from her computer screen and tipped her head. "Mmm-hmm." She smiled, her lips pressed together. "Both days."

I slid my phone across the counter toward her. "I'm looking for my sister. She stayed here."

Her eyes looked downward fleetingly. "We're not really supposed to talk about our guests."

"I understand." I felt the pressure of having this one brief moment to win her over. I slouched non-confrontationally, smiled weakly, and lowered my voice. "She's my little sister. She was here with a boy, they fought, he left her here. And we haven't heard from her in days." I left out Carmen's email. "I flew in this morning to look for her."

She looked at my phone again: this time her gaze lingered. "Really, we see so many people," she murmured and shook her head, but her eyes didn't leave the surface of my phone.

"The boy she was with." My voice lifted as it picked up speed, encouraged by her hesitation. "He said he left her backpack at the desk Wednesday morning. I just want to know if she picked up the bag."

She looked at me and bit her lip. My fingernails dug into the palms of my fists and I held my breath. I could see her weighing her options. "She picked it up."

My heart soared. "She did? When?"

"Wednesday sometime. My shift ended at three, so before that."

"How did she look?"

"She looked okay. Tired, maybe?"

"Oh my god. Thank you so much. You have no idea."

She nodded and looked around her, as if to see who might have overheard the exchange. I picked up my suitcase and moved away, not wanting to get her in trouble.

I was momentarily elated. I had proof that Charlie was alive on Wednesday after Isaac left. Where she went after that or where she was now, I had no idea. That part was somewhat deflating.

I checked into my room, set my bag down in the corner, and used the restroom. When I came out, I stripped the duvet from the bed and made a phone call.

My father picked up before it rang.

"Dad."

"Where are you?"

"The hotel. I just checked in."

"I told you to call me when you landed."

"I know. I'm sorry. Listen." I sat on the edge of the bed. "She picked up the bag. On Wednesday."

There was a whoosh of air on the other end of the phone. I felt his relief.

"So, here's the thing. I'm gonna go out in a minute and I'm going to show her picture to everyone in the hotel. But if I don't find her in, like," I shook my wrist, glancing at my watch. "Let's say two hours. If I don't get some kind of information, a lead, something, I'm going to the police."

"Okay. That makes sense."

"Yeah?"

"Yeah."

It felt good to hear. "I'll call you if I find anything."

I hung up and went out to the casino floor. I tried to imagine who would have seen her, stopping a dozen bored waitresses as they carried trays of drinks to gamblers. No one remembered having seen her; most seemed annoyed at my having crossed their paths.

And then, because it was in her search history, I crossed the street and went to Denny's.

As I stepped into the restaurant, I heard the specific ring tone I'd set for my father. Reaching for my phone, I was slightly annoyed. I'd told him I'd call if there was any news and there wasn't, not really.

I pulled out my phone and the hostess greeted me. I pressed a button sending the call to voicemail as I let her show me to a table.

She sat me in a booth and I ordered a coffee, handing back the menu. "Have you seen this girl?" I asked, holding out my phone.

She took the phone from me and pulled her glasses from the top of her head. Her hair was a deep cranberry, making it hard to guess her age. She could have been a hard-living thirty-five or a sixty year old who'd taken care of herself.

"She's my sister," I said, thinking it might make her try harder.

"She does look familiar."

As much as I gave Charlie crap about it – her thrift store irony and the oversized glasses she sometimes wore despite having perfect vision – she was memorable. It came in handy.

The waitress nodded and handed the phone back. "A couple days ago?"

"Do you remember which day?"

"It must have been Wednesday evening." It was only a few more hours of life, but I was grateful for it.

"Was she with anyone?" I asked.

"No, just her." She looked around the restaurant, seemed to take the status of the patrons' drinks: full up. She dragged a chair over and sat down. "Is she in trouble?"

"I hope not. She hasn't been in touch with any of her friends or family in days and I'm really worried about her."

"Oh, dear. I have a teenage granddaughter. They'll rip your heart right out. Her mother was no walk in the park, either."

"She's never done anything like this before." I felt like I was defending Charlie's reputation or refusing membership in a club for the families of troubled teens.

The woman nodded and covered my hands with hers. I know she meant it to be comforting, but I wanted to pull away. To be comforted was to admit defeat.

"Anything you can remember would be so helpful."

"She was sitting at that table over there? By the window?" She pointed to a table now occupied by a heavy, balding man. "And she was wearing a scarf like they do, those young hipsters. I just think it's so silly, you know. I mean scarves in Las Vegas? In April?"

I smiled. I'd made a very similar comment to Charlie not that long ago. On the coldest day in Tucson, no one needed a scarf.

I leaned forward. "Did she seem upset? Or, I don't know, worried?"

She squinted at the ceiling. "I didn't talk to her. That's not my section." She shrugged an apology.

I perked up. "Whose section is it?"

"Maria," she said, and I felt jarred by the familiarity of the name. It was a common name. Meaningless. Still, it set off an internal alarm. "But, Maria's off today. Sorry, hon, I wish I could be more help." She stood to go.

"That's a lot, really. Thank you so much."

"Oh, of course, honey. Good luck."

As she walked away, my phone rang again. I rolled my eyes. "Hi, Dad."

"I know where Charlie is."

"What? Did she come home?" I'd promised myself not to be annoyed if this happened. What was a wasted trip to Vegas in the scheme of things?

"No. You need to go get her."

part two - Charlie

6. Tuesday

I let him think it's his idea. He's had more to drink so I take the first shift driving, even though it's his car. He's really excited and chatty at first, but before an hour has passed, he's dozing.

I have the letter folded into a tiny square and tucked into the front pocket of my thrift-store flannel, pressed against my heart.

I should have left a note for Carmen at least. But that would mean she'd have to lie and lying has never been something Carmen was good at. Funny, since she's good at just about everything else. I've been copying her homework since the first grade.

I'd only known Carmen a few months when my mother left. I stayed at her house that weekend, eating huge bowls of ice cream and watching a marathon of Disney movies. I remember the borrowed smell of her pajamas with the strawberries on them. It was a clean smell, just unfamiliar. The whole house smelled different from mine, the pillowcases and furniture and bathroom soaps and kitchen spices.

Over the years, it got harder to put my finger on the difference, now that I'd spent almost as much time there as my own house. But that first weekend, the smells were so foreign and yet so reassuring. They worked so hard to convince me that everything was all right. It came as a surprise that when I returned Sunday night, my mother was still gone.

There were many more weekends like that one. Eventually, they stopped trying to coddle the motherless girl. That's when I really fell for them. Mrs. Rodriguez told me to call her Lydia, which I never did. In my head, she's Carmen's Mami. Carmen's Papi is the only one who calls her Lydia, though he usually calls her Mamacita and he kisses the back of her neck as Carmen and I mime a gag, pointing fingers in our gaping mouths.

Everything I know about Mexican cooking, I learned in the Rodriguez kitchen. My own father knows how to cook steak and order pizza. Anything that needs more effort than that requires my older sister, who makes meatloaf and tuna casserole. Olivia doesn't know a tamale from a chimichanga, and seems determined to keep it that way. She took French in school and what minimal Spanish she knows is spoken with an exaggerated white girl accent.

I don't dare turn on the radio because I don't want to wake Isaac. The thoughts in my head are loud enough to keep me from falling asleep on the long stretch of dark desert highway.

It takes effort for someone growing up in Tucson to know as little Spanish as my older sister, especially when you consider that she'd had six more years with our mother than I'd had. She must have to try pretty hard not to remember.

Almost as hard as I try not to forget.

The sky brightens by degrees. Isaac yawns and rubs his face.

"You never woke me to take over."

I shrug. "I didn't mind. We'll switch when we stop for breakfast. You hungry?"

"Yeah and I gotta piss."

"Can you hold it? I know a place but it's up further."

"I thought you said you'd never been to Vegas."

"I was really little. I didn't get to do any gambling."

I replayed the memory of that family vacation whenever I wanted to feel normal. We'd had so much fun that weekend, strolling along the main strip in our safe little cluster. I was perched on my father's shoulders, towering above the crowd. My mom and dad were holding hands and Olivia was allowed to walk just a few steps ahead of us. There was a man on the corner with a snake around his neck. People stopped to have their picture taken holding it. More men stood on the edge of the sidewalk, handing out post-cards. From my vantage point, I could see the scantily clad women in the pictures. My father held my mother's hand and my left foot; he didn't have a hand free for dirty advertisements.

We went to the Venetian to ride the gondolas. The canals were still relatively new then; it was the entire reason we'd taken the trip. My mother joked it might be the closest she ever came to Italy.

Before another year had passed, she was gone.

"Did you see the fountains at the Bellagio?" Isaac asks me now.

"I don't remember them, but I've heard they're really impressive," I say, though it's hard for me to imagine a bunch of light and water could be so interesting. A whole paragraph of the letter in my pocket is devoted to those fountains and I am still baffled by the waste.

The restaurant is different than I remember, but I'm sure it's the same place. Isaac thinks I have an amazing memory because he doesn't know I looked it up online days ago. They have a few dozen types of pie listed on a blackboard and I decide peach cobbler will make a good breakfast.

Isaac gets his eggs over medium, with sausage. He looks at the time on his cell phone. "Are your parents gonna freak when they find out you're gone?"

"It's just my dad."

"Oh, yeah."

"He leaves for work before I'd be up, but he'll probably notice my car's gone."

"You should have told him you were staying at Carmen's."

I shrug. "It doesn't matter."

"No?" His mouth is full. "Are you missing anything besides Ethics?"

"Just Anatomy. But I can get the notes."

Isaac nods and chews. He actually eats pretty heartily for such a skinny guy. I don't really know him that well, but we've made out a few times. We're dating, though we've never been out on a date, per se. Unless you count this.

So, I'm not sure what to do when the bill comes. When I reach for my wallet, I realize I don't have my cell phone. It's just as well.

"Oh, I got it," he says and I put my wallet away.

Isaac drives the rest of the way, which frees me to gawk out the window once we reach the strip. I go nuts for the pink lights of the Flamingo and beg to stay there. I tell him I like it because it's a bit of the old style Vegas surviving all the updates. That's not really why, but he agrees.

When we check in, he gives them his credit card. He carries my backpack down the long corridor to our room. We have a king size bed.

"Do you want to use my phone to call your parents? Just to let them know you're fine?"

"I told you: I don't have *parents,*" I snap.

He flinches. "Right. Your dad, I mean."

What an idiot. If he thought he was getting laid, he can forget that.

"If I call, he'll just ask where I am and then tell me to come home." I don't want him to know where I am and I'm done listening to him tell me what to do.

Isaac nods, knowingly. "Better to ask for forgiveness than permission," he says.

I make a show of how exhausted I am, get in bed with my clothes on and pull the pillow over my head.

When I wake, he's gone. Hotel window coverings block out all sense of night and day. I reach to turn the clock toward me; it says 5:17 and I lay in bed several more minutes as I puzzle out AM or PM. Neither one is good. I kick off the covers and go to the window, pulling the curtains back. Below, the daylight of the strip is fading into evening.

I go to the bathroom to pee. I catch my reflection in the mirror: smeared eyeliner and pillow creases on my cheek. How could I have slept so long? I do not feel rested.

Olivia would be getting out of work about now. No doubt my dad will call her. I can hear them saying how unlike me this is. They'll be so worried and it serves them right.

But Carmen. She doesn't deserve to worry. Maybe I can text her from Isaac's phone.

I get my toiletries bag so I can brush my teeth, wash my face and redo my makeup, which consists mostly of liquid eyeliner and mascara. I spend a little more time than usual sculpting my short, black hair into a spike that Olivia hates.

It's six o'clock before I leave the room.

It takes me a while to find Isaac; without my cell I can't text him. He's gambling at a table with three other people. Everyone has a drink and they're laughing. I approach slowly.

"Hey," I say when I'm standing at Isaac's elbow. He doesn't look up from his cards which makes me feel awkward, like people won't know we're together and will assume I'm just bothering him. "Whatcha doin?"

"Blackjack."

"Why didn't you wake me?"

"I figured you were tired. You did most of the driving."

This is true. "But you didn't even leave a note."

"I forgot about your phone. I was going to go back and get you at some point."

"When? You let me sleep all day."

He must hear the whine in my voice because he finally looks at me. "Geez, I didn't know it was my job to wake you up," he says, with a clear edge of annoyance. "There aren't exactly a lot of clocks around here. I sort of lost track of time. Okay?"

I realize that depending on my response, we could be in a fight. It seems a bit early for that.

"Are you winning?" I ask.

He shrugs. "Up and down."

"Have you eaten anything?"

"No." He's not even looking at me, so intent on his cards.

"Well, shouldn't we get dinner or something?"

"Why don't you play for a bit? You just got up."

I feel uncomfortable at the tables. The dealer feels like an authority figure, someone who will check my fake ID and tell me to call my father. I wander off to some slots nearby and play quarter machines. I win for a while. When I've lost ten dollars worth, I head back to the blackjack table to nag Isaac about dinner. I don't know what time it is, but my stomach is growling. This is turning out to be less fun than I'd imagined.

"I think there's a Denny's across the street." Isaac's willing to leave the table, which probably means he's losing.

I feel dizzy for a moment. "Not Denny's."

"The restaurants in Vegas are really expensive. And I'm getting low on cash."

"That's okay. My treat." I try to sound cheerful.

We find a Chinese restaurant on the second floor of Harrah's. It's out of the way and not so busy. I think the prices might be more reasonable than in some of the newer, glitzier hotels. Many of those restaurants are named for celebrity chefs and we don't even pause to read the menus by the doorway.

At dinner, Isaac sits on the other side of the table; our hands are intertwined in the center. His dark hair has streaks of green through it, but you can only see it in the light or if you know what to look for. It falls in his eyes and I'm itching to push it back.

He looks up. “Are you having fun?”

I smile. It isn’t exactly a false smile, but it doesn’t feel like the whole truth. “Mm-hm.”

“I never went on a trip with a *girl* before.”

“I never went on a trip without adult chaperones.”

He laughs. “Really?”

I nod.

“Not even camping?”

“Nope.”

He squeezes my fingers. I think I should tell him about the letter in my pocket and why I really wanted to come here.

Suddenly at the next table, the waiters gather to sing happy birthday to a yellow haired woman covered in glitter, wearing a tube top. Isaac sets down his menu to sing along. I do not. I hate restaurant birthdays. Anyone who knows me knows better than to inform the wait staff it’s my birthday. Which it actually is next week.

I’ve never liked birthdays. I always have to celebrate it to make my father and Olivia happy, but I would much rather that the day passed without notice. Carmen’s the only person in my life who knows this about me, the only person who understands why.

I turned seven two weeks after my mother left us. I remember the false levity of that day. Before she left, I’d gone hunting for my gifts, found the stash at the back of her closet, including the doll I’d been begging for. On my birthday, the doll was all I got out of the group of presents I’d found that day. The rest had been thrown out or given away and replaced by things my father had picked out: a kite, a red and white Chinese finger trap, play-doh. But the doll had stayed.

I wonder if my mother had purchased my gifts knowing she wouldn’t be around to give them to me or if her leaving had been spontaneous. When she left, packing up the contents of her closet while Olivia and I were at school, did she come across this group of presents at the back? Did she consider that at the very least, it was horrible fucking timing?

We order a Pupu platter and a scorpion bowl. I pay with cash. I have a credit card, but my father’s name is on the account, which means he can check the activity online. I know because he does this a lot, even when I’m not missing. He isn’t sneaky about it; he’ll nag me if I don't pay the full bill each month, which I nearly always do. Because I know he'll be checking it.

On the walk back, Isaac gets more money from the ATM.

"Isaac, how much have you spent?"

"It's no big deal."

"Are you just going to gamble the whole time?"

"It's Las Vegas. What did you think we'd do?"

"We could go dancing. I heard of a club that sounds cool."

"Nah. I don't dance."

"Come on." I pull him closer as we walk. "Guys don't really have to dance. I'll just dance up on you. It'll be fun."

He slows. "Look. The fountains." He stands behind me with his arms wrapped around my body. "How about we gamble in this casino for another couple hours. Then we'll head to this club of yours."

I sigh. The ten dollars I threw away on the slots is really all I can bear to waste. "Fine. Go gamble. I'll come find you when it's time."

"What are you gonna do?"

"I'll stay for the light show." I nod my head toward the fountain. "I'll pick up some post cards. You'll just be in this casino? At a blackjack table?"

Isaac nods.

"I'll find you."

He kisses me then, and I think about how the rest of the night will play out, our sweaty bodies grinding to the pulse of Lady Gaga and some strobe lights. The scorpion bowl has left me with a pleasant buzz and there will be more drinks at the club. It will be quite late when we collapse into bed and I'll be able to lose myself there as well.

I watch him jog across the street, the crowd swallows him and I just see the back of his head bobbing its way inside. I sit on a bench.

Vegas is beautiful at night. Everything that seemed dirty during the day is now in shadow. The competing marquees are evidence of an electrical bill I don't want to contemplate. The excess and wastefulness of this city is an affront to my principles of environmental conservation. And yet, in spite of that, I love it.

Tonight, they're playing Singing in the Rain. It starts slow but as the music swells, the water shoots higher. At a pause in the music, the fountains cut off and the lake goes placid and dark. The onlookers gasp with collective surprise. When it starts up again, they *ooh* and *ahh*. The streams of water are like dancers; they sway to the rhythm. They seem to skip and swing and high kick. The fountains are mesmerizing; she's right. I can see getting lost in thought here.

My mother lives in this city. Four days ago, I got a letter from her and my head is not done exploding. I've told no one about it, not even Carmen.

The letter is written on purple stationary that I imagine she bought just to write to me. Who has stationary these days? It was dated April 17th, thirteen years to the day since she left. It began with an apology, of course. And just as I was wondering to myself if Olivia would be receiving a similar letter, I read this bombshell:

Years ago, I tried to get back in touch with Olivia. She wanted nothing to do with me and I understood. She asked me not to contact you and I respected her request for as long as I could.

I'd spent years of my childhood motherless because this woman had decided to leave. And then I spent more years that way because Olivia decided not to let her come back.

So that's why I'm not calling home.

At the next show, the water embodies Michael Jackson's heartbreak as he shouts: "What about us?" The fountains jump and snap and leap and moonwalk. When the music stops, everyone claps and I leave the fountains behind me. I walk down the sidewalk and stop at a few little shops along the way. I consider getting postcards like I said I would, but this isn't really that sort of vacation. When the crowd starts to thin, I turn around and head back.

I never responded to the letter and I still haven't decided what I'm going to do about it. Isaac doesn't know why we're really here. He thinks we're being spontaneous.

The heat that made my flannel shirt seem like an odd choice during the day has dissipated. I hug myself in the breeze as I cross the street.

I have imagined stalking my mother and going home without speaking to her or confronting her publicly in some really embarrassing way that's bound to get her fired. I've even fantasized about starting a random conversation with her to test whether she can recognize me after all these years. I expect thirteen years mean less change for a grown woman than they do for a child.

I should probably tell Isaac what's going on.

This is what I'm thinking as I spot him sitting at a table. All the stools are taken. He looks up at me as I approach. "I'm winning!"

"That's awesome!" I imagine he'll be buying the drinks at the club.

The hand ends and he pulls the chips toward him, then taps the table and the dealer hands him new cards.

"Are you almost done?" I ask.

"No, I can't leave right now. I'm on a streak."

"But you said we'd go dancing."

"We will, but." He studies the cards in his hand, tosses two to the dealer. "It just doesn't work that way. I've got to ride the wave."

He doesn't look at me to see that I'm scowling. He pulls out his wallet and hands me a twenty. "Get yourself a drink."

And I take it, because the alternative is storming off and having to buy my own drinks. Who does that punish?

I sit at the bar and order a martini. It looks really cool with its distinctive little glass and its olive on a spear, but it tastes disgusting. I finish it anyway. Isaac knows where to find me, but he hasn't shown up. I twist on the bar stool and flash a smile to the man sitting next to me. It would serve Isaac right to find me getting cozy with this guy. He looks older, mid-twenties. He's wearing a crisp, white, button-up shirt tucked into jeans. He's a little bit beefy, in a good way, like I couldn't push him over if I tried. Holding my empty martini glass, I slide the olive from its plastic spear with my teeth. He's looking back at me and I can tell he likes what he sees. I start leaning toward him, slowly, as his girlfriend returns from the bathroom and I swivel back. This time, I order a rum and coke.

The letter arrived on Friday. The handwriting on the envelope looked like Olivia's and I wondered why she'd send me mail when she lived about seven minutes away. Then I saw the return address in Nevada and my stomach tightened with the possibility of it.

The truth is, I'd waited my whole life for this letter. I hadn't known where it would come from; most of my fantasies had her back in Mexico where she had family. When I turned eighteen, I'd been especially diligent about mail collection. I googled her name periodically, but it turns out that Maria Flores is a very common name. She's on facebook and twitter. She's a glass artist, an actress, a director of career services. She lives in Boca Raton, Orange County, Colorado Springs.

I'm halfway through my drink when an older guy leans in and says something I can't hear over the music and the crowd. I regret making confused eye contact because he leans in closer, his lips brushing against my ear, his long, graying hair touching my face "Let me buy you a real drink, sweetheart."

I roll my eyes, slightly insulted. "No, thanks. I'm fine," I yell.

He shrugs and turns away.

I sat on the couch in the living room that day, tearing the envelope with trembling fingers. I held my breath, a buzzing in my ears, thinking *pleasepleaseplease* as the room swayed and became tinted sepia.

And there, below my full name in cursive, she'd written: *My baby.*

The trip to Las Vegas was inevitable then, a foregone conclusion. As I continued to read, I realized I wouldn't be taking it to Olivia, or my father.

Which meant I couldn't tell Carmen, the one person in my life who would know what this meant, who would be happy for me, who could help me think it through.

When I finish my rum and coke, I regret turning down the offer from the long haired Sugar Daddy. I wonder if I can take him up on it now, but I see he's moved on, chatting up a blond. It's just as well. I don't want to talk to anyone. When I ask the bartender for a shot of Patron, my tongue feels a bit clumsy. I down it and settle my bill

"What time is it?" I have to shout over the crowd.

The bartender looks at his wrist. "1:30," he shouts back.

Isaac's at the same blackjack table. I can't tell if he's winning or losing and he doesn't notice me as I walk by.

The shot doesn't hit me fully until the walk back. I stumble in the hallway, struggle with the key card and fall into bed.

7. Wednesday

In the middle of the night, I wake in the pitch black to a rustling noise. Disoriented, it comes to me slowly where I am. I turn on the bedside light and find Isaac in the corner, elbow deep in my backpack.

At first, we just squint at each other. I'm waiting for him to explain himself. When he doesn't, I go first: "What the fuck are you doing, Isaac?"

"I didn't want to wake you."

I push the covers off and sit on the edge of the bed. As soon as I'm upright, my head starts pounding. "What are you looking for?"

"I was going to pay you back."

"What?" My wallet is in the nightstand, thick with twenties from the ATM in Tucson. None of which are to be pissed away by this douche bag. "I thought you were winning."

"I was."

"You blew through all that money already?"

"That's how it works. Sometimes you're up; sometimes you're down. You've just got to ride it out and not be a pussy."

"Jesus. Do you have a gambling problem or something?"

"Of course not. Don't be so dramatic."

I think back to the way he'd talked about this trip. All I had to say was that I'd never been to Vegas and he'd fallen over himself suggesting ways to remedy that. Immediately.

"I'm not giving you any of my money, Isaac."

"Fine. We're checking out tomorrow." He heads for the door.

"Where are you going? You have no money."

"Don't worry about it."

The door clicks shut. I get up and slide the inner latch. If he wants back in, he'll have to knock. I go to the bathroom and fill one of the short glasses by the sink. I drink it down, refill it, drink another. I don't have time to be worrying about this. I have my own stuff.

But he doesn't come back. I get up at nine and take a long shower. I wear my least wrinkly grey shirt with the dark jeans I've been wearing the whole trip. The plaid scarf I drape around my neck has a little blue in it if you look close. I slick my hair back and do my makeup, then think better of it and spike it.

I told him I wanted to stay at the Flamingo because of the pink lights of the marquee, because it's one of the strip's few old school casinos to survive all the new development. It's also a short walk to the Denny's.

I have done my research.

Outside, the sun is so bright. It permeates the darkness of my clothing. Just the walk across the street makes me wish I'd packed shorts, even though I never wear shorts. Even in the middle of summer in Tucson. I have scrawny, stupid chicken legs. I haven't worn shorts since junior high.

At Denny's, they have the air conditioning cranked so high that my outfit is justified.

I order breakfast off the plastic menu even though it's nearly noon. Breakfast anytime. I look around the restaurant. Women with big hair and tired faces pour coffee and tug at their skirts, taking orders from loud families and large men. She isn't here.

When my waitress stops to ask if I need more tea, I counter: "Do you know if Maria's working today?"

"Maria?" She pauses and refocuses her attention on me. "I think she works the evening shift, honey."

I thank her, rub my palms against the top of my thighs and get back to my pancakes. When Carmen and I were younger, we supported each other through several strict diets, but in the end I just didn't have the will power. Carmen did. Whenever I watch her counting the seven tiny morsels she allows herself at mealtime, or hear her retching in the bathroom, or catch a glimpse of her twig-like, brown thighs, I feel awash with guilt at having deserted her.

Of course, I know I'm not supposed to feel guilty for not having an eating disorder, but it is what it is. Carmen has followed me into every hare-brained idea and dysfunctional relationship I've ever had, never judging, always supportive.

I try to be there for her, but she knows I don't really understand. I've read enough books to know that I can't talk her out of it. I cringe when someone who doesn't know tells her she looks great when she's at her tiniest. What is it with people and their need to encourage any sign of female deprivation? I'll compliment her hair, her tan, her outfit. Never her weight. Sometimes she fills out and I think she's being healthier, but that's not necessarily the case. She might be in a binging phase. The guilty purging and laxatives would follow. She has good days and bad days.

I go back to the room after breakfast, but my key doesn't work. I spend several minutes trying. I slide it fast, slow, upside down. But each time, the red light flashes.

At the counter in the lobby, I stand on the shiny white marble floor and explain. I'm expecting a new key card, but the blond tips her head at me, looking like I'm an object of pity.

"Paulson?" she asks.

I nod. That's Isaac's last name. I recognize it when she says it, but I'm not entirely sure I could have remembered it right away on my own.

"He checked out at noon. Left a backpack for you to pick up."

I keep my face blank. I try not to look hurt or surprised. She's wearing a pink cardigan and a little pearlescent barrette to hold back her perfectly smooth hair. I don't want her feeling sorry for me. She reminds me of my old Flight Attendant Barbie. If anything, I should feel sorry for her.

She asks to check my ID first and I'm about to hand over the fake one when I remember. For this, I have to be myself. She passes the bag to me and wishes me a great day with her big horsey smile and improbably white teeth.

I pull my backpack over both shoulders and wander through the casino. I don't feel like gambling, but at least there's AC.

I can't believe Isaac checked out. I look for him at the blackjack tables and when he isn't there, I feel like I might actually start to cry. I don't know where else to look for him and, for the first time, the loss of my cell phone begins to seem like a catastrophe. I feel lost. My breaths are coming quick and shallow and the terror that I may be having a panic attack increases the likelihood that I'll have a panic attack.

I struggle to get my backpack off and sit on the floor, against the wall. I hadn't wanted to come here alone. When I finished reading her letter, I'd gone to my closet and started packing. I'd carried this backpack around for days while I formulated a plan.

She'd included her phone number, but I couldn't call her. None of the fantasies I'd had about finding my mother involved an awkward telephone conversation. I wanted to see her face.

I hug my backpack to my chest. Surely, Isaac would not have left me here. I keep the blackjack tables in my line of sight and imagine him looking for me. I'll be easier to find if I stay in one place. When he finds me, we'll have one of those amazing talks that change everything. He'll admit he has a gambling problem and I'll tell him about my mother. I still haven't decided whether I want to see her. We'll figure it all out together.

I wish, as I always wish, that I could talk to Carmen. She'd know what to do. I wish I'd told her from the beginning. I wish that we had made the trip together. I hadn't been sure she'd come with me, though, that she wouldn't tell her parents what was going on. Carmen was only good at keeping a certain kind of secret. If she thought she was protecting you, her silence was impenetrable. But she couldn't make people worried. Not on purpose.

So there was Isaac. I didn't want to go by myself.

And here I was: by myself.

I sit there for more than an hour. Every time someone stops to try to sell me a drink or ask if I'm all right, I pretend to look for something in the bag. I wish I had my cell phone to stare at. No one bothers you when it looks like you're texting. Of course, if I had my cell phone, I could call Isaac. Finally, I remember that I wrote down the section where we'd parked when we got here yesterday. It's all I can think of that connects us. Maybe he's left a note for me there, under the windshield wiper. Maybe I should leave a note for him. I pull the scrap of paper from the front zippered pocket and head for the elevator.

In the parking garage, I find a green Prius where his Firebird should be.

I stand there, looking between the scrap of paper and the parking space, unable to take it in.

I want to think of a reason he might have moved the car. I can't. I stand there for a long time, shaking with rage and trying not to cry. When I get home, I'm going to kill him. But, right now, home feels further away than a seven-hour drive. It feels like a totally different universe, a place I knew in another lifetime.

When I'm done staring at the offending Prius, I take the elevator back to the casino. I consider getting a room for the night, but I don't want to use my credit card and I don't have that many twenties. A motel down one of the side streets might be cheaper.

It doesn't even occur to me to go home. As much as I keep telling myself I haven't decided to see her, I can't just leave now. I'm so close.

And, it turns out, she's the only person I know in the city.

The sky is just as I remember. A light blue, purposefully surreal and unnaturally perfect. The light is honey-tinged and voices echo and carry as if through a tunnel. I watch a young family in one of the gondolas. The two girls are closer in age than Olivia and I. Their parents look so tired.

Had my parents looked that tired all those years ago when we were here, riding the gondolas? My mom had been talking about that ride for weeks. I'd expected more from it. It was slow and dull and before I knew it, over.

I'd never known my parents were unhappy, or that she was. I suppose, if you're lucky, no six year old has an awareness of that sort of thing.

That night, I go back to Denny's. This time I ask to be seated in Maria's section. I notice her immediately, taking an order at the next table. She looks a lot like Olivia, only shorter and darker. Mexican. Olivia must have hated that.

I'm trying to think of what I'll say when she comes over. I imagine I could just order and wait to see if she notices me. Before I can think of anything clever, she turns from the couple next to me and talks to me over her shoulder.

"Be right with you," she says, and she runs off and disappears into the kitchen where I can only assume she's putting in the order she's just taken.

She didn't really look at me, but I'm horrified by the possibility that she won't recognize me. Before, when I'd considered that happening, I'd imagined it in terms of her embarrassment. Shame. But faced with the reality that my own mother could forget my face, could be unable to claim me as *hers*, I feel completely disconnected from the world. Orphaned. It's a whole new kind of abandonment.

I touch the hair at the back of my neck. It's so short.

My mother arrives at the table. She starts to pull a white notepad from the apron at her waist as she looks up at me. She blinks. Once. Twice. She has dark eyes and long eyelashes. She doesn't seem to be wearing mascara, or any other make-up really. Her dark hair is tied back in a ponytail. If I didn't know she was in her forties, I'd guess she was much younger.

"Charlotte," she whispers, and I'm so relieved I start to cry.

The pad goes back into her apron, next to a row of straws. She sits down across the table from me and clasps her hands under her chin, like she's praying. She doesn't touch me.

I cover my face. In the fantasies, I never cry. I make her cry. I take a breath and force myself to stop. I drop my hands and look across the table at her.

She smiles. She seems calmer than I want her to be and she isn't crying. She pulls a paper napkin from the metal dispenser on the table and hands it to me. I press it against my face quickly, embarrassed.

"I got your letter," I say, stupidly, because I don't know where else to start.

She nods. "You're so beautiful."

I feel my face flush. It seems like we're having different conversations, like she isn't even listening to me.

"I had to see you," I say.

And she nods, like *of course*. "How long can you stay?"

I feel like I might cry again when she says that. I shrug and my anger at Isaac helps me push past the lump in my throat. "My ride left me here so I'm kind of stranded."

"Left you here?" She sounds appropriately offended for me. She passes that particular test.

"We had a fight and he took off."

She shakes her head. "That's awful."

I shrug again. "So I have nowhere to stay."

"Did you call your dad?"

I shake my head and glare at her to convey that she's asked the wrong question.

She tries again. "You can stay with me. Would you like that?"

In the end, I order a burger and eat while she arranges to leave work early.

We don't talk much in the car, which is a little strange. I feel like all the difficult conversations of my adolescence took place in the car. Olivia or my father driving, the safety of not being forced to make eye contact. It made it easier to ask for permission to go to a concert on a school night or persuade Olivia to take me to the clinic for birth control.

Instead, we listen to NPR and she offers me a Tictac from the little box she finds in one of the cup holders. I accept and she opens the box with a snap and shakes a miniscule green mint into my palm.

"Thank you," I say.

The truth is, this entire reunion isn't going quite like I'd planned. I don't like being in the position to need a favor from this woman. Not that getting a ride and a place to stay makes up for the previous thirteen years of zero rides and never even knowing what state she was in, but it has thrown me off. I'm a polite person. When I thank her, she says, "Oh, it's nothing," and I think: *I know.*

I made my First Confession when I was nine. I had plenty to confess; I had a fascinating, much older sister and I snooped through her bedroom every chance I got. She had tiny lace underwear in all different colors when she was just fifteen. Often, my confessions sounded more like things she should be confessing, a long list of her secrets, many of which were incomprehensible to me.

Olivia wasn't Catholic, though. I imagined this was why she held grudges while I could let things go. I cultivated a forgiving heart. I prayed for it. I always knew this day was coming and I wanted to be ready. I imagined bestowing my forgiveness upon my mother as she sobbed at my feet. Or perhaps something slightly less dramatic.

But not this. I'm sitting in this car, pinching myself, as if I'm being driven around by a celebrity. As if I am so lucky.

Neither my father nor my sister had anything nice to say about my mother. They didn't like to talk about her, so we didn't.

The only person I talked to about my mother was Carmen. I told her the same stories over and over again, whispers in the dark as we fell asleep. They were my most treasured collection: The way she painted my fingernails and toenails with a bottle of hot pink polish, whenever she was doing her own. How she'd color the page opposite the one I picked in the coloring book. All the summer days she drove Olivia and me up Mt Lemmon, to escape the heat. The time she made cupcakes for lunch and it was our secret.

There weren't many. She left when I was just starting to form memories.

She lives in a trailer park called Shady Valley. I'm pretty sure Nevada doesn't have those. It's irony or wishful thinking or someone's weird sense of humor and I'm still thinking about whoever must have thought of it when she parks in front of a yellow trailer with white trim, a single wide.

She flips on the lights and I follow her inside. I've never been inside a house trailer, so I'm a little surprised to find that it looks pretty much like a regular home. I think I'm expecting plush carpeting and wood paneling on the walls or something campy, but the floors are laminate or tile and the walls are painted a soft gray.

There's a plastic laundry basket on the couch. She scoops it up and disappears into the back bedroom, returning with sheets and blankets. I move to help her but she waves me off so I just watch as she tosses the sheet away from her body and it falls slowly and crookedly. She bends to straighten and tuck, a strand of dark hair coming loose from her ponytail. As she wrestles a pillow into the pillowcase, she asks if she can get me anything to eat or drink and I tell her I'm fine.

"Let's talk for a bit," she says and she sits on the loveseat, motioning for me to sit on the couch she's just made up.

"Does anyone know where you are?" she asks.

"Just you." I smile like maybe this is funny, but she frowns.

"You could use my phone," she says.

"No, thanks." I set my jaw.

She nods.

"How long have you lived here?" I'm curious, but mostly I just want to change the subject.

"A little more than a year."

"And before that?"

"Lots of places." She pulls her hair from the elastic and it cascades around her face. She's very pretty. Olivia shouldn't lighten her hair so much. "I have a cousin in California so I went out there at first. Then I followed a boyfriend to Seattle. I was in Colorado for a while. I was even in Phoenix." She looks up at the ceiling and scrolls through her memory. "Seven years ago? When I talked to Olivia. She'd just turned eighteen."

She bends down to remove her shoes. "I went to talk to her at the house when I knew your dad would be at work. You weren't home, but Olivia was worried that you'd come back and see me. She wouldn't even let me in the house. I had to plead my case from the front step."

I imagine what it would have been like to come home and find her like that. To have had my mother back at twelve instead of all these years later. Who the hell did Olivia think she was?

"Why didn't you come to see me when I turned eighteen?"

She leans forward, elbows on her knees. "I was in no shape, sweetheart," she says and then she gives me the longer story. This wasn't in the letter. She'd been drinking most of the years since she'd left. Some years she doesn't even remember. She'd been in jail for nine months and before that she'd been basically homeless. When she got out, she made several attempts at sobriety; none of them stuck.

When I was eighteen, she was living with some guy in Reno and they drank together whenever they were awake. He beat her up pretty bad and she started to get sober in the hospital. But that recovery lapsed too.

"I remember being in a bar in April. It was April 17th, the exact day I left all those years ago. I hated that day. Whenever it came around, it was like an anniversary of the worst thing I'd ever done. It was usually an excuse to get really, really black out drunk. But this time, I took the sign different. I decided to make it the day I stopped drinking. I got my year chip from AA last week." She digs into her purse and hands it to me.

"Wow," I say and I turn it over in my fingers.

"So now that day means something good." She's looking at me and smiling with tears in her eyes.

I hand the chip back. She blinks and puts it away.

"What are you missing?" she asks.

"What?" The question throws me and my potential responses compete with each other and go unsaid. I'm relieved when she clarifies.

"Back home. What are you missing? School? Work?"

"Just some classes."

"So you're in college?"

"A sophomore."

"That's so great. I never went to college."

She looks up at the clock above the television. "I have to be up early for work. I'll try to take off on Friday so we can really spend some time together, but I can't skip out tomorrow without someone to cover. Is that okay?"

"Sure."

She stands. "I'll put some fresh towels in the bathroom. Help yourself to the fridge. I'll leave my number on the counter if you need anything."

I nod.

"You'll be okay?"

"Yeah, I'll just watch tv or whatever."

"Okay. I'll be home for dinner. I'm so glad you're here."

She reaches out and touches my face lightly. It's the first time my mother has touched me since that day thirteen years ago, when she sent me off to the school bus.

I nod. "I'm real tired."

8. Thursday

My mother stands over me for a long moment as I keep my breathing even and pretend to be asleep. She carries her shoes out the door and locks me in and drives away and only then do I get up.

I start with the medicine cabinet. Inside, I find toenail clippers, dental floss, a bottle of Vitamin C. I open the bottle and shake the pills into my hand. They're identical orange circles with the letter "C" carved into the top. I place the bottle back inside, careful to twist it a quarter turn, just as I found it.

There are mis-matched, raggedy towels folded neatly in the cabinet under the sink. In her closet, I find two sleeveless sundresses, one slinky red Lycra number, several cardigans, eight blouses and three pairs of shoes: pink sneakers, black heels and brown flats. Folded sweaters take up all the shelf space. She has a murder mystery in the bed, open with the pages face down. She's about half-way through. The jewelry box by her bed has a gold bracelet with her initials, a string of red rosary beads, and three condoms.

The freezer is much better stocked than the refrigerator. There's ice cream and waffles and TV dinners galore. In the fridge, there's 1% milk, half a bottle of RC cola, store brand maple syrup and a bag of baby carrots.

If there's alcohol in the house, I can't find it. She doesn't even have Advil.

She's left a selection of breakfast bars on the kitchen counter. There's no computer, but there's cable. I take a Raspberry Crunch bar to the couch, switch on the television, and start channel surfing.

Just after noon, a blue truck parks in front of the house and a man walks up the front steps and knocks on the door. I lower the volume on the television.

"Charlotte? Maria sent me to check on you." He takes off his sunglasses and holds a hand over his eyes as he peers in the front window. He's looking right at me.

At my house in Tucson, all the shades would be down and if I didn't know someone was coming over, I wasn't to open the door. It had always been that way.

Here, I can't pretend no one's home. I open the door because it seems rude not to. I'm wearing those same jeans and the T-shirt

I've slept in, no bra. I fold my arms across my chest and stand in the doorway.

"Charlotte! Hey there, it's Ben. I'm friends with your mom."

"Oh, hi," I say and keep one arm awkwardly over my chest as I stick out my hand. He shakes it.

"Maria called me from work. She didn't think there'd be lunch fixins, so she asked me to take you out." Ben's a good-looking guy, with short, dark hair and a goatee. He looks to be in his late twenties, maybe thirty. He's wearing jeans and a white T-shirt with a logo on it. T&J Construction. He has a tattoo on his bicep, disappearing under his shirtsleeve so I can't tell what it is.

"Oh, that's okay. I'm fine." I remember my manners: "But thanks." I start to push the door shut.

"W-w-wait!" he says and he looks so confused I feel bad for him. But really, what was my mother thinking? She's forgotten the first rule of parenting.

I open the door again and smile apologetically. "Ben, I really appreciate the offer, but I can't go to lunch with you. I don't know you." Taking off to Vegas without warning, staying in a hotel with a boy he never met and drinking with a fake ID pale in comparison to what my dad would think of me getting in a car with a stranger. This thought nearly makes me reconsider.

"But I know your mother."

And I barely know her. I don't say it, but I think my facial expression conveys the sentiment.

Ben takes a few steps back down the stairs and scowls. He puts his sunglasses on the top of his head and scratches his goatee. Then he looks up at me and beams. "I'll just go down the street and get some subs. We can eat at the picnic table over there." He motions across the way, under some shade trees.

I consider this. It seems to be in keeping with the spirit of the law. The picnic table is in sight of several other trailers and there are people walking around, adults home in the middle of the day. I am starting to get hungry. "I have some money," I say, to signal my agreement.

"No, no, I got it." He doesn't wait for me to say anything more. He jumps back into his truck and pulls out before I can lock up. Once he's gone, I feel silly. I've acted like such a child, as if I'm in danger of being kidnapped. He knew my name; he'd been sent by my mother. I was following some kind of childhood script of obedience.

My father and I had a secret code word. If someone ever tried to convince me he'd been in an accident and had sent them to get me, I was supposed to ask for the code. To this day, I've never told anyone what that secret word was, not even Carmen. It drove her mad.

If my dad was in an accident, it would probably be Carmen's parents to come for me anyway.

While Ben's gone, I run to the bathroom and put on a bra and a short-sleeve top that's tight across my chest. I spike my hair, brush my teeth and reach for my eyeliner as I hear three short horn bursts in the drive. There's no time for eyeliner.

Across the way, I find Ben setting the picnic table with plastic flatware. "I'm sorry. I didn't realize 'til I got to the place that I never even asked what you like."

He has a ham and cheese and an Italian and lets me choose. I take the Italian.

"Is Coke okay?"

"Of course. Thanks. I'm sorry about before. I must seem paranoid."

"No, I understand. Girls have to be careful. Guys have the luxury of forgetting that."

"How do you know my—" I clear my throat. "How do you know Maria?"

He hesitates and a shadow falls across his face. "Uh, we met at church."

"Really?"

"Well." He takes a long pull on his straw. "We met in the church basement. You know Maria's in AA, right?"

"Oh, yeah. She showed me her chip."

"Oh, good. Phew! I didn't want to break confidentiality. But, yeah, that's how we met. She's so proud of that chip. She's come a long way."

"Did you know her before?"

"Oh, no. We've just talked a lot. That's what you do in AA. Talk. Tell your stories. You get to know people pretty well, pretty quickly, in AA."

It makes more sense, somehow, that they're AA friends. They don't seem like they'd have a lot in common otherwise. "So I guess you know all about me."

"A little. I mean, I know how much it means to her to have you here. She feels so bad that she has to work today."

"I don't mind."

He reaches across the table then and pulls my arm toward him. I'm startled until I see he's looking at my tattoo, an image of the Virgin on the inside of my forearm. He holds my wrist tenderly, my arm pinned gently to the table.

"This is beautiful," he says.

"Thanks. I sort of designed it myself."

"You did?"

"I mean it's based on other ones I'd seen," I say quickly. "But it was my drawing that I gave the tattoo artist." Carmen's cousin Lola had given me the family discount. She said my drawing was so good I should consider getting a job at the tattoo parlor. I remember thinking how much my father would love that.

"That is *so* cool," Ben says and my face still feels warm as he lets go of my wrist and reaches for his sandwich.

"What's this?" I indicate his bicep by touching my own.

He pulls up his sleeve. It's a woman's name. Karen. "The ex." He shrugs. "It seemed like a good idea at the time."

I try not to laugh.

"Nothing says 'I used to drink too much' like a bad tattoo."

"You could get it fixed. Change it into something else."

"What else do you think it could be?"

"Hmm." I squint at it. "I could sketch up a few designs."

"Really? That'd be awesome. So, you sticking around for awhile?"

"I guess." I'm not sure how long *awhile* is, but it seems vague enough to apply.

He pulls his phone out of his back pocket and glances at the time. "I need to get back to work." He starts putting the empty sandwich wrappers in the bag.

"Oh, let me clean up." I take the bag from him and stuff it with my paper trash. "What do you do?"

"I build houses. It's so weird, all the empty homes around and they never stop building. That's me: Ben Parker, part of the problem."

"The problem?"

"Oh, you know, urban sprawl. There are already too many people living out here and they just keep coming. When the Colorado River dries up, we're all screwed. But, until then!" He grins and holds his arms aloft in a mock-cheer.

I frown. "So what do we do?"

He steps over the bench. "Do?" He smiles at me like I'm a naïve, amusing child.

I try to laugh off my idealism. As if there's a solution to all of life's problems. Something simple like signing a petition, holding a sign at a rally. I carry my armful of trash to the dumpster as he drives away.

In the kitchen pantry, I find spaghetti and a jar of sauce. I set the table, turn the jar upside down and pound it against the counter. I love the satisfying pop of the lid opening with the casual twist of my wrist. When I see her car pull in, I throw the pasta into the boiling water.

"What's all this?" she says as she comes through the door.

"It's nothing," I say. "You were working all day so I just thought I'd do something to thank you for letting me stay here."

She sets her purse on the counter. "You didn't have to." She reaches out and touches my shoulder.

I stand there, awkwardly, unused to her touch. "I know."

She drops her hand to her side. "Well, it smells delicious."

"Thanks." I turn to give the sauce a stir. I switch the heat down.

"What do you want to do tomorrow?" she asks. "We could go back to the strip and I could give you a grand tour. There's a rollercoaster on the roof of the Stratosphere."

"I'm pretty over the strip." I shrug. "No offense. What do you usually do on your day off?"

"Sometimes I just go to the pool." She slaps her forehead. "Oh, I'm such an idiot. I should have given you the keys. I'm not a very good hostess."

"That's okay. I don't have a swimsuit anyway."

"You can borrow one of mine."

Involuntarily, I make a face. Borrowing bathing suits makes me as squeamish as borrowing underwear.

She laughs. "Or we can pick up a new one at Target?"

I pull a strand of spaghetti out with a fork and blow on it. "That sounds fun."

She helps me locate the colander and steps back as I pour out the water and breathe in the steam. She gets glasses down from the cabinet and fills them with water and ice cubes from the freezer. We're doing these everyday tasks as if we're passing a tray full of breakables back and forth. I suppose it will just take time.

She sits down and I serve the pasta onto our plates. "I'm actually surprised you found anything to cook in this kitchen. Ben said the two of you had subs?"

"Yeah. That was really nice of him."

"Ben's a good guy."

"You're AA friends?" I turn to lift the sauce from the stovetop.

She hesitates.

"It's okay," I say as I turn back. "He told me. He sounded really proud of you." I pour the sauce on her plate, then mine.

"That's Ben."

I put the empty pot in the sink and sit down across from her.

"The program really saved me," she says. "It saved us both I think. The idea of giving it over to a higher power: 'let go and let God.' It sounds like a small thing maybe, but it's been so huge."

"No. I don't think it's a small thing."

It's quiet. I wish I'd thought to turn on a radio or something. My mother looks up from the plate of food I've cooked for her. "We used to go to church as a family, but it got to be too much work," she says. "We stopped when you were just a baby. I regret that."

That's what she regrets. "I go to church," I say, twisting and twisting the spaghetti on my fork.

"You do?"

I nod, taking a bite.

"And Olivia?"

I shake my head. I'm not even sure Olivia believes in God. She can hardly disguise her contempt for Catholicism. She's even worse when it comes to people who take The Bible literally. "I go with my best friend and her family. Every Sunday."

"So do I. Every Sunday." My mother talks with her mouth full, excited. "Since I got sober. Maybe we can go together this Sunday." She pauses and reaches for her glass. "If you're still here."

"Sure." I don't think The Bible is meant to be taken literally. There are too many direct contradictions: "eye for an eye" or "turn the other cheek"? Depending on your political agenda, you can use it to defend whatever position you already have. The Bible is really just a mirror. If you use it to defend something hateful, it's because you're a hateful person.

Out the window behind my mother's head, the sun is going down. The sky is pink. "Did Olivia know you had a drinking problem?" I ask.

"I'm not sure. I don't think so." She lifts her glass. The ice cubes crash together.

"Did you tell her when you went to see her that time, when she was eighteen?"

"She didn't really want to hear anything I had to say. I don't blame her. I went to talk to her in person and I think it came as a shock. That's why I decided to write to you first. To give you time to think about it."

"When you contacted her, I would have been twelve."

She nods.

So, instead of living six years without a mother, I'd gone nearly fourteen years. All because Olivia decided. "And she didn't want me to see you."

"She was pretty adamant."

"It wasn't for her to decide."

"Well, to be fair, you were still a child."

"Did my dad know?"

"I don't know. Not unless she told him."

"And then you started drinking again. After she sent you away?"

She hesitates. "I don't blame Olivia for that. Those were my choices."

"At least you got choices." She apologized in the letter, but she still hasn't done it out loud.

We're quiet again, chewing. Again, I wish for the solace of a radio. After Olivia moved out, I started leaving the television on whenever I was home alone, for noise. My father would come home from work to find it blaring in an empty room, while I was studying in the kitchen. He'd grumble about the electric bill.

"Do you have internet?" I ask.

"No, but you can check your email on my phone." She stands and begins to rummage through her purse. "Here."

She holds it out to me and I take it.

"Honey?" she says, tentatively. I look up at her. "Don't you think you should call your dad or Olivia or someone?"

"No."

"They must be so worried. Come on, you can use my phone."

"You lost the right to tell me what to do a long time ago."

She presses her lips together and looks at the floor, nodding. After a few moments, she says goodnight and goes to her room, mentioning something about the book she's reading. It's not even 8:00.

Carmen has left a series of increasingly panicked emails. In the last, I count seven exclamation points and it's written entirely in caps. I should have left her a note at least. I'd planned on texting her, but I hadn't planned on losing my phone.

When we'd dieted together in junior high, we kept a record of our weights and added up our daily calories and wrote it all down in a Lisa Frank notebook with a unicorn on the cover. On the day I got lightheaded in the locker room after gym class, I left the journal on the island in the kitchen where I knew Olivia would find it. I couldn't rescue myself, but I knew I could count on Olivia.

I was twelve. It was September. Olivia had turned eighteen that summer and decided I didn't need a mother.

I can't say anything to Carmen that will tell her where I am. I imagine Olivia and my father must be breathing down her neck. Her parents too.

It's hard to type on this thing. I'm used to my phone with the slide out keyboard for texting. On this one, I have to press the number 2 three times for the first letter of her name. In the end, all I manage is this:

"Carmen , I'm okay. I wish I could tell you more. I will explain everything soon."

9. Friday

My mother tiptoes into the dark kitchen and starts the coffee maker. When I get up, she apologizes profusely for waking me. I hadn't really been sleeping, though. The ruffled curtains in the living room are just for show.

I cleaned up our dishes from last night, washing the uneaten portion of hers down the disposal. I felt guilty about it and then I felt mad at her for making me feel guilty. Then mad at myself for being mad at her. I'd been trapped in this spiral most of the night, kicking off the sheets and waking later, chilled, unable to find the edge of the blanket.

We still haven't had a moment where she apologizes and I forgive her. Nothing official. My appearance seems to signal forgiveness, as if it doesn't need to be said. As if it can be assumed. I want to forgive her. I do. That's what I planned. But I feel like it's a question and I can't just give it over until she asks.

So it's surreal to sit at her table eating waffles and making small-talk. To sit in the front seat of her car and thank her for the tic-tac as we drive to Target.

She buzzes down her window and apologizes as she lights a cigarette. I haven't seen her smoke until now. It occurs to me that she was on her best behavior before and now she's getting comfortable enough to be herself.

"Are those the only pants you brought?" She motions to the dark jeans I'm wearing. I've been lucky so far that I haven't spilled anything on them.

"Yeah."

"You can borrow some shorts. I know you're taller than me, but I think I have shorts that would be okay." We stop at a red light and she takes a long drag, holding it in.

"I hate my legs."

She lets her breath out the window and turns to me as the light changes. "Your legs? What's wrong with your legs?"

"They're just gangly."

"What?" She presses the gas and we lurch through the intersection. "Are you crazy? I'd kill for long legs like yours."

I shake my head.

"You know what I think?" She pulls on the cigarette again, creating a pause in the conversation that makes it seem like it might not be a rhetorical question. She turns her head away from me and speaks on the exhale. "I think someone made fun of your legs when you were a kid and you're still hanging onto it." She turns to look me over, long enough that I shift in my seat and wonder who's watching the road. "But you're all grown up now, Charlotte, and you have those long, beautiful legs. Show them off!"

I laugh, noncommittally. I am all grown up.

"Well, it's up to you. I'll just put some out for you when we get home."

"This one's cute," she says and she lifts a one-piece from the rack. She holds it out to me and I take it. It's bright and patterned, a sort of multi-colored confetti.

My smile is false, but she can't tell. The next one she picks has pink flowers on a white background. I hate the cut of a one-piece, the bare skin of the uppermost inner thigh. This skin was not meant to be seen by anyone other than a boyfriend or a gynecologist.

I gravitate to the two-pieces. There's a ruched black skirt that is more conservative, but still sort of sexy. I toss it into my cart.

"Oh, I like that," she says, and she takes the one-piece from my hands and puts it back. "That'll go with any top. You can mix and match."

An older woman walks past us and throws my mother a knowing glance. We look like any mother and daughter swimsuit shopping.

I choose a patterned tank top with a halter neckline. The medium looks right. Close enough. The idea of trying things on makes me itch. Growing up, I'd always gone shopping with Carmen and her mom. We'd come out of the dressing room together and pose while Mrs. Rodriguez straightened our collars and checked our hemlines and made sure enough of our bodies were covered.

At the check out, my mother takes her purse from her shoulder and looks prepared to pay. I refuse. I lay my purchases on the conveyor belt: the bathing suit, a three-pack of cotton underwear, a sketchpad and some good pencils. I hand over some bills, along with the last fresh ATM twenty. The next time I pay for something, I'll have to put it on my credit card and they'll know where I am. The prospect is slightly thrilling, like I'm a criminal who longs to get caught.

I've been gone for almost five days, depending on when you start counting. Olivia and my dad must be beside themselves.

A few weekends before I got my mother's letter, Olivia had taken me to lunch at La Cocina. She mispronounced it as she always did, calling it "la co-chee-na", which is Spanish for pig. I'd been correcting her for years; it's "la co-see-na", kitchen.

We sat at one of the metal tables in the courtyard to the left of the stage. At night, there'd be a band and the courtyard would be glowing, its palm trees wrapped in white Christmas lights. For now, there was a woman playing the harp. At intervals, she'd stop and the lunch goers would clap politely.

Olivia and I had salads and milkshakes. I got strawberry, she got mocha, and we shared. I searched the koi pond for the two happy turtles who lived there.

Olivia brought me here to tell me she'd broken up with her boyfriend of six years. I put on a brave face, but Rick had been part of the family so long that I'd taken him for granted as a permanent fixture, like Carmen.

"Why?"

"We're of an age," she said vaguely, brushing her light brown hair out of her face. Her fingernails were filed neat and bare. Mine were short, covered in chipped red polish.

"What does that mean? You're twenty-five."

She sighed like it was tiresome having to explain things to me. "If Rick wants a family, he needs to start dating women who want the same thing."

"You don't?"

"Kids? No. Do you?"

"Yes. Why do you seem so surprised?"

"I don't know. You're always talking about conservation. Do you really think this planet needs more humans?"

"Maybe I'll adopt." It's easier for me to imagine never getting married than never being a mother.

Olivia nodded, her mouth full of salad. I had her approval.

"So am I just never gonna see him again?"

"Who?"

"Rick!"

She laughed. “Of course you’ll see him again. Things will just be weird between us for a little bit. Anyway, let’s talk about something else. How’s school?”

“Fine.”

“Do you think you’re going to stay at Pima?”

It was nice of her to ask it that way. Originally, the idea was that I’d transfer to a *real* school next year, but I hadn’t really given it much thought lately, which I’d need to do if I was going to be sending applications. I’d dreaded this conversation, expecting a fight.

“Yeah, I think I’ll stay,” I said and Olivia just nodded again and moved on.

My mother wears a red bikini with a blue towel tied around her hips. She has a canvas tote bag on her shoulder filled with copies of Us Weekly and bottled water and Coppertone. She’s loaned me a pair of flip flops for the walk to the pool. At the gate, she takes the key from the stretchy band at her wrist and lets us in.

I follow her, my own towel, yellow, knotted at my waist. She chooses two lounge chairs and angles them for tanning purposes. She pulls off her towel, steps out of her flip-flops and heads to the shallow end of the pool.

“No sense putting on sun screen yet,” she says. She steps into the water, slow but sure and walks out deeper. When it’s over her waist, she submerges and swims underwater the rest of the way. She pops up and clings to the edge. “You coming in?”

“Not yet,” I say. There’s no one else here, but I have to get my bearings first. I like to wait until I’m so hot, I can’t stand waiting anymore. Only when it becomes a physical imperative can I shed my swimwear self-consciousness.

My mother pulls herself out of the pool and stands at the foot of our chairs. She twists her hair into a tight cord, the water streaming off of her. Her breasts are bigger than mine and her flat stomach is another denial of motherhood.

She reaches for her towel, presses it quickly to the front of her body and then lays it on her chair. “You better go in. Otherwise, what was the point of getting the swimsuit?”

“I’ll go in,” I insist.

She raises her hands as if to say *okayokay* and sits down next to me. She rummages through her bag and tosses me the sun screen. “You first.”

I obey, starting with my legs.

“What’s this for?” She pulls out the notebook and the new pencils I put in the bag before we left.

“I’m going to sketch up some tattoo designs for Ben.”

“For Ben?”

“He mentioned that he’d like to cover the one that’s on his bicep. I said I’d come up with ideas. I drew this one.” I hold out my arm to show her the Virgin, black on a red background.

She holds my arm at the elbow and uses her other hand to trace the design on my forearm. “Wow,” she says. “Did that hurt?”

“A little.” I remember how my right leg kept twitching the whole time. I got used to the needle, but that was disorienting. “First, she did the outline. That felt sharper, worse at the wrist. The shading was more like gnawing.”

“How long did it take?”

“A few hours.”

Her eyes open wider. She lets go of me, shaking her head as she turns away. “Oh, I could never!”

I shrug. “Sure you could. I’ve heard childbirth is a lot harder.”

“Oh, honey, they give you drugs for that!”

We laugh together and I trade her the lotion bottle for the notebook. I notice she didn’t try to sell me on the result of childbirth: the baby bliss. I remember seeing the pictures of her in the hospital when I was born. I always thought she looked happy when she wasn’t.

She starts rubbing the sunscreen into her dark skin. “So did Ben say what kind of tattoo he wants?”

I open the notebook to the first page. “Not really. He just wants to cover his ex-girlfriend’s name.”

“Ex-girlfriend?” She pauses and cocks an eyebrow and I wonder if I’ve accidentally revealed something she didn’t know.

“Karen?”

She nods. “Ex-wife.”

My eyes widen.

“Did he call her his ex-girlfriend?”

"He just said 'ex' and I assumed. He doesn't seem old enough to have been married."

"Ah." She lies back and closes her eyes. "We're all old enough."

"I suppose."

I start by drawing the Karen tattoo as it is. The thing about covering a tattoo is that it's trickier than just drawing over it. You have to sort of hide the old design in the new one, incorporate it.

The past is never really gone.

"Don't you have homework or something?" she asks.

"No."

"No? I've never heard of a college student without homework."

I sigh. I should have asked Ben what kind of tattoo he'd want. I realize I don't know him well enough to make something up.

"I'm worried about you falling behind."

"Well, it isn't for you to worry about." I close the notebook. "I'm all grown up, remember?"

"Okay. I'm sorry," she says, but again she's apologizing for the wrong thing.

"It's fine." I stand up. "I'm going in." I jump right into the deep end and sink to the bottom. My primal scream comes out in a swarm of large bubbles.

When I get out of the pool, my mother has the towel around her waist and she's stepping into her flip-flops. There's still nothing to make for lunch, so she's going to the grocery store. She invites me along, but I opt to stay where I am.

I recline the chaise and close my eyes against the sun. As the gate clangs shut, my mother calls out to remind me to reapply the sunscreen. I call back, offering polite promises, but I make no move to do so.

I stretch my legs out in front of me. My knees seem to bulge from the middle of skinny limbs, like a giraffe. My mother was right before when she said that someone made fun of them when I was a kid: Olivia. We were watching a nature program and a baby giraffe toddled into view.

"Oh, look at its legs! It's Charlie!" I can still hear her. It was so long ago, I'm sure she wouldn't even remember. But I do.

Once I'm sure my mother's too far away to see, I reach for the sunscreen.

It's my idea to invite Ben to dinner, but my mother seems happy to include him. Perhaps a full day in my company has been more than she bargained for.

We meet him at a steakhouse nearby. We get there first and I know he's come in behind me when my mother's face lights up. She stands and they embrace and he holds her a little too close, a little too long. He presses his fingers into her waist.

I feel the heat rising to my face and I look away. Ben pats my shoulder and says my name. I force myself to look up at him, smile, say hello.

He slides into the booth beside her and I see them for what they are: a couple. I wonder how I've misjudged his age. I thought he was so much younger than her. I knew he was older than I am, but I thought we were closer in age than they could be. Sitting next to each other, their age difference is not apparent.

"So how was your day?" Ben asks.

I reach for my water glass and let my mother answer. When she starts telling him about my sketches, I feel a second wave of embarrassment. I'd been trying to impress a boy who was only paying attention to me as a favor to my mother.

"Did you bring your notebook?" my mother asks.

"No." I make myself talk to them, to ignore the irrational urge to pout or tantrum. "I really didn't end up coming up with anything. I didn't know what you'd like." It's out of my mouth before I realize how true that is. I feel like such an idiot.

The waiter comes. We haven't even looked at the menus. Ben and my mother order iced teas. I think about the fake I.D. in my wallet and imagine their faces if I ask for a beer. But that would be immature. I hate that maturity is such a struggle for me sometimes. The impulse to lash out for petty slights: it's not attractive. I know this.

I order a coke and lift my menu as the waiter turns to go.

"I'm really impressed with your talent," my mother says. "Did you take art classes in school?"

I look up from the menu. The crazy feelings are receding. "Some."

"I can't even draw a straight line." Ben says.

"Funny, neither can I," I say. "I always sucked at geometry graphing, but these aren't straight lines." I hold my arm out in front of me, looking it over.

We read our menus and when the waiter returns we order ribs and burgers.

"So, how long are you staying?" Ben asks and my mother's head snaps toward him.

"Um, I hadn't decided."

"Well, you're welcome to stay as long as you want," my mother says quickly. "I love having you."

We say goodbye in the parking lot. Ben and my mother hug chastely, fooling no one. When we get back, we watch Jimmy Fallon on the couch. When she stops laughing, I realize my mother has fallen asleep. I look at her more closely than I have since I got here. I haven't really been able to as long as she was looking back.

You would think all those years drinking would have aged her more quickly. Or, I would. I would have thought that. But her face is mostly smooth, just the requisite creases at the corners of her mouth, visible even when she's in repose. One line across her forehead. Olivia probably has as much to show for herself at twenty-five.

She's beautiful, my mother. If she'd raised me, would I wear less makeup? Would I have learned to take pride in my long legs? Would I be more confident that my beauty was like hers or would I have felt diminished in her shadow?

She opens her eyes as I'm watching her and she startles, but says nothing. We stare at each other for a long moment and then she yawns, stretches, and goes to bed, making more misguided apologies. She has an early morning.

10. Saturday

Sweaty, I shove the pillow from my face and check the clock. I've somehow managed to sleep through sunrise and my mother leaving for work. It's after ten.

I shower and eat quickly to compensate for the late start. My mother has left the laundry quarters on the table in the kitchen along with a mesh laundry bag, a jug of detergent, and a folded up pair of shorts.

I've never used a Laundromat before and I'm a little nervous about it. I'm relieved when I unlock the door and push it open to find it empty. When I don't know what I'm doing, I prefer not to have witnesses. The lights flicker on automatically and the heavy door slams behind me as I hoist the laundry bag onto the closest machine.

I'm sure I can figure it out; I've seen it done on television. I lift the first three lids to find clothes plastered to the inside of the washers. A fourth machine is empty and I toss my clothes inside.

I'm not so spoiled that I don't know how to do laundry at all. Olivia taught me that when I was in grade school. The biggest difference I see is the quarters. I fit them into the spaces and give the metal slot a shove. I select my cycle and press start. When it begins to hum, I pretend I never had any doubt.

Growing up, I'd never had the sense that my father was a single parent. It isn't that I thought of Olivia as a mother, but she'd always seemed like another grown up, a more accessible, relatable one.

She taught me to do laundry, how to fry an egg. She was the adult who took me out driving when I was practicing for my license – she simply had more time than my father did. Olivia was in charge of the schedule and any change in the routine had to be run by her for approval.

When she moved out, it hit me. I barely knew how to talk to my father without Olivia to act as the ambassador.

I sit on top of one of the idle washing machines and open a magazine across my lap. The dryer in the corner is spinning. Through the window on the front, I watch a speedy rotisserie of striped boxer shorts.

When I was younger, I never had trouble talking to my dad. He was like an oversized playmate. We'd wrestle and play Monopoly and go on bike rides. He always laughed at my jokes. As I got older, it actually felt like I outgrew him. I became more interested in other things. One of those things was Olivia.

My older sister became much more interesting around the time she started shutting her bedroom door. Suddenly, I was forced to knock and wait to be granted permission to enter. The space had never seemed so sacred and mysterious until then. That's when I started snooping and "borrowing" – a lipstick, a pair of dangly earrings, those ridiculously impractical suede ankle boots. Not until she begged to go places alone did I feel the urge to follow, secretly if need be, eavesdropping, watching, mimicking.

Olivia was cool. She'd been popular and good at school. She was focused and made decisions without second-guessing. She was precise and careful and deliberate. She'd wanted to be a physical therapist since as far back as I could remember and so that's what she'd become. She didn't take shit from anyone. I'd seen her shout down a shopkeeper three times her size because she didn't like the way he talked to me. Olivia was fearless.

I have never yelled at anyone in my entire life. Unless you count Olivia, and you really shouldn't. Sisters yell at each other. It doesn't mean anything. In fact, I think it only means something when they stop yelling. That's when something's really wrong.

As I'm moving my laundry to the dryer, someone knocks on the window above my head. When I look up, Ben waves manically with one hand. In his other hand, he holds a bag from the sub shop.

I twist the handle and he pushes the door open.

"No one answered at the house so I called your mom. She told me to check here."

"You brought lunch again," I say, stating the obvious. Suddenly, I wish I was wearing long pants.

"I was in the neighborhood."

I start the dryer and decide to come back for my clothes. The digital counter says I have fifty-nine minutes.

Ben carries the detergent on the walk back. It's just past noon and already hot; the day will continue to heat up until sometime after three.

I unlock the front door and sigh with relief at the air conditioning. Ben puts the lunch bag on the kitchen table and jokes that he's allowed inside now, a promotion.

"I guess I'm not a stranger anymore," he says and I consider this. Lately everyone feels like a stranger, even the people I've known my whole life.

I get the drink glasses down from the cabinet and turn toward him. "Why didn't either of you tell me you were dating?" I blurt out. I say it with confidence, like I know for sure. But I'm still sort of hoping I'm wrong. When he doesn't deny it, my heart sinks just a little bit and I hope he can't see it on my face.

"It's new," he says.

I nod and put the glasses on the table.

Ben sits. "You're not really supposed to have romantic entanglements your first year of sobriety. Some people bend that rule, but your mom didn't want to cut corners. When she committed to AA, she was all in."

I sit down across from him and pull the subs from the bag. Like mirrored images, we unwrap our sandwiches. I don't ask him more about what sort of tattoo he'd like. The idea has lost its charm now that I know he isn't interested in me in the way I'd thought. It's not like I really wanted anything to come of it, but it changes the vibe to know he just thinks I'm some dumb kid.

"Would you ever consider going to Al-Anon?" he asks.

Startled, I look up.

"It's for family members."

"I know what it's for," I say and it comes out more irritable than I mean it to. I shrug. "I never really lived with an Alcoholic."

He pauses. "Didn't you?"

I feel my face flush as it dawns on me. Of course. For some reason, I'd assumed the drinking came after, a way to quiet the guilt. "I was really young when she left," I say quietly.

"Well, it's not just for that," he says quickly, noticing my discomfort. "My little sister went for awhile. She was so young when my dad left she hardly remembers, but she got to see me at my worst."

"How old is she?"

He squints at the ceiling. "Thirty-two?"

So he's older than thirty-two.

"I put her through a lot. I still feel guilty about it. My mom too, but I think Amy got the worst of it. She was always trying to save me even when the rest of my family was keeping their distance."

"Tough love."

"Yeah. My older brother still hardly talks to me."

"How long have you been sober?"

"Six years, three months and … seventeen days."

"Congratulations."

"Thanks." He takes a big bite of his sandwich and chews. "Anyway, Amy said it really helped her. AlAnon. I think my mom went a couple times too. See, I quit a few times before it stuck. And we'd get to a good place and then I'd relapse and we'd have to start over."

"Do you think my mom's gonna relapse?"

"Oh God no, that's not what I mean at all. Your mom's doing great. It's just that dealing with an alcoholic can take a toll, even a recovered one. It can help to talk to people going through the same thing."

"Help?"

"With whatever feelings you're struggling with."

"I'm not struggling."

"Okay."

He goes back to his sandwich and I go back to mine.

Struggling is the wrong word, I think. It's more like I'm stewing, trapped in filthy bath water, paralyzed as everyone adds their bucket to the mix. My mother. My father. Olivia. I'm not struggling; I'm paralyzed. I can't move. I can't get out.

When Ben leaves, I go back to collect my laundry and find that someone beat me to it. Nothing's stolen, but some stranger has touched my under things and piled my clothes on the top of an empty machine.

I spend the afternoon watching CNN. There's a forest fire in California and they're running non-stop coverage of it, making me wonder what more relevant news story they're trying to distract us from. If I had my phone, I'd search the internet to find out what was really going on in the world. As it is, I watch the blazing footage as it's repeated and repeated, building a familiar queasy numbness.

Every generation has that tragedy that defines them. The Kennedy shooting. The Challenger Spaceshuttle explosion. For

Olivia, it's 9/11. I was only five. I have no memory of it, not even the mysterious grown up whispers and changing of channels. Nothing.

For me, it's the Aspen fire of 2003. Mt Lemmon burned for a month the summer I was seven. My mother left in April, my birthday was in May, and the fire was in June. By the end of the summer, when we were allowed up to survey the damage, the town of Summerhaven had been ravaged. The trees were bare and black. Our favorite restaurant, the one that made the best blackberry pie, had burned to the ground. The old woman who owned that little shop decided not to rebuild. I heard she took the insurance money and the recipes and move to Ohio.

My mother liked the strawberry rhubarb. My dad teased her that she only got it so she wouldn't have to share. None of the rest of us could stand rhubarb.

We used to drive up the mountain nearly every day of summer. If it was 100 degrees in the city, it'd be 80 degrees up there. We collected pinecones in the shade and ate peanut butter and jelly sandwiches on picnic tables. On weekends, my dad would come along and we'd have pie.

The summer the mountain burned was the first summer without my mom and she hadn't taken us up at all yet that year. The smoke was visible from our house, large billowy clouds covering the Santa Catalina mountain range. After dark, you could see the flames glowing red in the black night.

When my mother's car pulls into the driveway, I snap off the television and begin folding my laundry. It feels deceptive and I'm not sure why I do it.

She sits on the loveseat and takes off her shoes, rubbing the arch of her left foot. "How about a pizza?" she suggests.

"Tired?"

She leans against the couch cushions, seeming to dissolve. "So tired."

She gets a second wind after the pizza. We agree to go to church together in the morning and then I remember I have nothing appropriate to wear. Her face lights up and she pulls me to her closet. I can tell without trying it on that her short sundress will be scandalously short on me. I take the longer one into the bathroom. It has pink rosebuds on a blue background and falls just below the knee. On my mother, it must be mid-calf.

I stand in the doorway and she pronounces me beautiful.

She reaches for the red dress and holds it out to me.

"Not exactly church appropriate," I say, raising an eyebrow.

"I know, but just for fun." She shakes the hanger and I take it, laughing, and run to the bathroom.

I pull the first dress off and step into the red one. Even without doing the zipper, it's tight. I can't really see myself in the mirror above the sink. In the bedroom, my mother stands behind me in the full-length mirror, zipping me up.

"Woah," she says, her chin on my shoulder.

"Did you get this for an occasion?" I ask.

"Actually I bought it on a whim. I've never even worn it. You should take it. It looks better on you anyway."

"Oh no. I couldn't." I look down at myself. I can't imagine where I would wear something like this.

"Please. Take it." We're looking at each other in the mirror. It seems so important to her.

I slide my hands down along my hips. "Okay," I say quietly and my mother smiles, satisfied. She turns away to look out the window.

"Did you write me that letter as part of your AA program?" I ask.

"What?"

"Was it part of your *amends*? Something you had to do?"

She frowns. "Charlotte, amends aren't like that. They're not something you do to pass the test. The things in my life I feel genuine sorrow for, leaving you and Olivia—" She shakes her head as tears fill her eyes. "There's no greater sorrow in the world."

I hug her then. It is as if someone's pulled the stopper on the tub just as the water was starting to fill my mouth. The anger is still there, but receding. I hold her tightly as it begins to drain out of me and I finally know for certain that I'm not going to drown.

part three

11. Saturday (Roger)

Leaving Olivia at the airport felt as if I'd lost one child down a well and tossed the other one down in a vain hope to retrieve the first. As I set my keys on the table just inside my front door, I felt bereft. Like I'd lost them both.

Which was irrational and simply stupid. Olivia would be fine. She was always fine.

Olivia had been my easy child. Not knowing what to expect, I'd been especially concerned about my abilities to raise girls alone. When Maria left, Olivia had been approaching adolescence and I braced myself for the inevitable transformation, the sulking and pouting, the crying and yelling, the boyfriend I'd hate, the whiff of pot on those friends who were a bad influence. But none of it came. Olivia got good grades, was popular and involved in school, but never had time to date or get in trouble. She took care of her little sister, cooked and cleaned. On a practical level, I hardly noticed Maria was gone.

(On another level, I felt Maria's absence in every breath, every wincing use of the pronoun "we" to describe feelings and plans and positions that were now mine alone.)

Olivia was so good that I was lulled into the false sense that things would be just the same with Charlotte.

Charlotte was emotional; she always had been. Even as a baby, she'd been so sensitive to noises, we had to tiptoe around the house when she was sleeping or there'd be hell to pay – between her wailing and Maria's fury. As a toddler, her tantrums were magnificent. She had an outrageous, high-pitched shriek that felt like an ice pick in your temples. For years, we were unable to eat in a restaurant as a family. We stopped going to church after the first few attempts landed me gratefully in the vestibule, jiggling a fussy infant while Maria sat with Olivia. I didn't mind missing out on the priest's monotone monologue. I had converted to Catholicism when I married Maria, though when I really thought about it, I was probably more of an atheist. I didn't think about it all that much. Maria didn't like sitting in the pew with just Olivia; she said it defeated the whole purpose of going to mass as a family. I had thought the point was to listen as the priest rehashed the Book of Matthew and encouraged women to obey their husbands. But I was a closeted heathen; what did I know?

Maria took exception to the phrase "terrible twos", as Charlotte's behavior only worsened when she turned three and didn't seem to get any better until she was five and began spending half-days at kindergarten, where she finally seemed to find an outlet for her superhuman energy.

Her close friendship with Carmen Rodriguez had been a life-long romance. They met the year Maria left, as first-graders. Lydia and Jorge were a godsend (even to an atheist) that year. I met them for the first time only after I had become a single parent in one sudden, unexpected evening. I was able to hold it together in front of my daughters because of the weekends they took care of Charlie, the evenings we ate dinners Lydia dropped by (always some combination of meat, cheese, and tortilla I never knew by name). Those moments of reprieve gave me time to fall apart in private. To get my feet back under me. To adjust.

Charlie's fierce love for the Rodriguez family rivaled my own.

If Maria had had her way, Charlotte would never have been born.

Before having children, Maria had always wanted to be a mother. Afterwards, not so much.

It was clear when we brought Olivia home from the hospital as a newborn. I hadn't noticed before that, at the hospital. Everything was so hectic and there were so many people visiting with congratulations and taking turns holding the baby. Maria was always smiling, I remember. In retrospect, I imagine a blank quality in her eyes, but I can't be sure if it was really there already or if that came later. I certainly didn't notice it at the time.

After everyone had left us, Maria wanted nothing but sleep. She was so tired and she did not want to breastfeed, as she'd wanted before the birth and had discussed with the nurses at the hospital. Now, she shut herself alone in the bedroom and directed me to find the bottles of formula they'd sent home with us.

If I had been the one to balk at changing diapers, to cringe at the sound of the baby crying, it would not have been thought strange.

The womenfolk would have rolled their eyes at me; I had be shooed from the room and laughed off as another useless man. But it's so unnatural for a mother to lack interest in her own child, in every babble and cry. All the firsts. I remembered it all. I often wondered what Maria remembered.

It must have been post-partum or something. It didn't occur to me at the time, all those years ago. If people were talking about it then, I don't remember.

Olivia was five when Maria got pregnant again, a surprise. A pleasant one I thought, but, no. Clearly, no. Maria said she couldn't go through it, not again. That's what she kept saying: "Not again, not when I just got my life back." Olivia had begun kindergarten that fall.

I didn't know what she meant at first. She was frantic and I tried to reassure her. People always said the second child was easier, didn't they? But Maria would not be calmed. She spoke of making an appointment at a clinic, all her Catholicism out the window. We had one of those intense fights, where you say the worst kind of things to each other, things you can never take back. She was screaming and breaking dishes and pulling at her hair.

"I'd rather burn in hell for eternity!" she yelled when I reminded her abortion was a mortal sin. I wasn't even religious, but that was my baby she was talking about.

That night, Olivia staggered into the kitchen in her pajamas, crying, scared. We stopped yelling at each other then. I carried Olivia back to her room and Maria left the house. She came back before sunrise and got Olivia ready for school. We never spoke of it again.

Charlotte was born in May. I took three weeks off work and when I felt like I had to go back, I often took her with me. The practice was mine, so there was no one to complain. My receptionist had grandchildren who lived across the country. She loved Charlotte and seemed to understand that there were complications at home. By the time Charlotte was mobile, Maria was behaving more like herself and Olivia was getting old enough to help out.

The tragedies in my life have always caught me unprepared. When I was twenty-five years old, my parents were in a fatal car crash. At the time, I was in my last year of dental school. I had a room mate who was also in the program, and we didn't share very much else in common. I had recently met Maria at a party, got her number, and hadn't thought about her again. The shock of my parents' death changed the entire trajectory of my life. One year later, I had graduated from dental school, I was a husband and new father.

That is how you deal with tragedy. Bad things happen in everyone's life; it's how we decide to react that determines what kind of person we are. Wallowing is a choice. You can wallow or you can work to change your situation. If you're unhappy, fix it.

I used the money I inherited to buy an existing practice from a retiring dentist. Along with the office, I got all the equipment and staff. I let everyone go except for the receptionist. Those first few years, I only worked three days a week to save on overhead. These days, I had appointments booked solid from 8am to 6pm. I had patients who refused to see anyone else. I treated their parents and children. I was especially popular with older folk.

My wife leaving me was a different kind of tragedy, and perhaps one I should have seen coming, but I didn't. If anything, I'd begun to feel that life was settling down. Charlie had started first grade. She and Olivia rode the same bus to school. Maria and I fought less, made love every Saturday after the kids were in bed, quietly. We settled into a routine.

She left on a Thursday. She had been gone for hours before the girls came home to an empty house. Olivia called me at the office and I had Judy tell her I'd call her back when I was finished with my patient. It was close to four when Olivia answered, her voice trembling. I tried to reassure her that her mom was probably just running errands and got caught up. But no, Olivia insisted, I had to come home. When I hesitated, she let out what she'd been trying not to say: the closet and bureau were empty. There was a note on the bed.

When I came home, Olivia was sitting on the couch with her hands in her lap. Charlotte was playing in the back yard. The glue on the envelope was still sealed. I sat on the bed as I read the words in a blur, a rush. I skimmed for the gist, knowing I'd have to return to the living room, face my daughters and an uncertain future. There'd be time for a deeper reading later. There'd be years.

"Mommy needed a break," is what I told Olivia that night, and we settled on another, kinder version for her little sister. That weekend, Charlie went to Carmen's house and I tried to spare Olivia any outward signs of my terror and grief, as I made phone calls and hit dead ends and ultimately gave up. There weren't that many people to call. She had a grandmother who lived in Mexico without a telephone. She was estranged from the aunt who'd raised her. In all our years together, Maria had never liked to talk about family. I had thought our rootlessness was something we'd understood about each other. But I may have been wrong about that, too.

Her letter did not express doubt. It didn't suggest she needed a break or time to think. In that letter, Maria revised everything I'd thought I'd known about our marriage, about who she was. "I'm done," she said. "I'm sorry, but I'm done."

It occurred to me later, what had made Olivia think to check for her mother's clothes, to open the closet door? Had she, at twelve, seen something coming that I had not?

My usual weekend routine involved reading. Nothing nonfiction or informational; I got enough of that during a workweek. I liked to read something with entertainment value: some John Grisham or George R. R. Martin. An escape.

But on this day, I couldn't focus so I flipped on the television and compensated for my own judgment of it by finding something educational. The Discovery Channel was showing some series on Planet Earth, meant to make viewers care about it. As climate change became something measured in the present rather than forecasts of a dire future, I watched the deniers go from the "it doesn't exist" camp to the "there's nothing we can do about it" camp, having never set foot for a moment in that complicated space in the middle where the rest of us lived.

In the abstract, the extinction of the human race troubled me not at all. The planet didn't need us any more than it needed the dinosaurs. Perhaps the next species to give it a go would be more considerate of their host.

But as a father, I worried about the world my daughters would inherit.

A tampon commercial came on and I reached for the remote, muting it. When I was young, you could still watch television in mixed company without the humiliation of advertisements for boner pills and adult diapers.

When Olivia was thirteen, she'd come to find me early one morning. She was dressed oddly, in baggy dark sweatpants I'd never seen her wear. She was scratching her arms and not looking at me.

She stammered her way through telling me and I was so furious. Maria had left that April. Maria, the mother I had chosen for my children, the mother who should have been there to listen and advise.

Instead, it was me she came to, pale and embarrassed. My heart broke for her.

I rushed out to the store, assuring her I'd be quick and there was nothing to worry about. I was a grown man in the feminine hygiene aisle. I'd certainly been there before; I'd been married for fifteen years. But I couldn't remember the brand she'd preferred, didn't know whether to get tampons for a young girl or the pads with wings or without. I ended up buying one of practically everything, my shopping cart full of little pink boxes.

I put all the purchases in the hall bathroom and took Charlie to the mall, to give Olivia the house to herself while she sorted it all out. I wanted to spare her as much embarrassment as I could. It was the only thing I had to offer.

In retrospect, I probably wasn't supposed to treat it as something she should have been embarrassed about. I must have made the worst parenting mistakes with Olivia, the one who hit all the milestones first, but she turned out okay. It was Charlie I worried over. Not just now, because she was suddenly gone, but always.

They say kids are resilient and that described Olivia to a T. But not Charlie. Charlie got her feelings hurt and held onto it. She'd remember something I'd said when she was little, throw it back at me in an argument about something totally different. I could never defend myself, unable to recall whether I'd said it or not, wondering how she had such infinite access to ancient resentments. She could sulk for days before she'd tell you what was wrong and when she finally did, it was often some imagined slight, an issue with my *tone*.

I unmuted the television in time for an advertisement for a program that aired a week from tomorrow. The date took my breath away. On that Sunday, Charlie would turn nineteen. I refused to believe in a world in which she would not.

I Birthdays were a big deal in our house. We celebrated with big crowds in the back yard or a bowling alley or the church basement. Lydia Rodriguez had helped me put together an authentic Mexican coming-of-age for Charlie's fifteenth. It was so fun, it made me regret that Olivia hadn't had one. I had never been separated from either of my children on their birthdays. I tried to shake the dread that crawled icily up the back of my neck. Surely, she'd be back by then.

I snapped off the television and the house fell silent.

The phone rang that evening. I was expecting a call from Olivia, an update on how things were going. But this was an unfamiliar number. My heart leapt: Charlie.

"Hello?"

It was quiet.

"Charlie?"

"No. Sorry." It was a woman speaking so softly I could barely hear her. She cleared her throat. "It's Maria."

"Maria?"

"Charlie's with me."

"What?"

"She's safe. She came to see me."

My mouth was suddenly dry. "Where are you?"

"I'm in Las Vegas. I sent her a letter last week and she came to see me. To talk. She's been here the last few days. I told her to call you, but she wouldn't. I just wanted to let you know she's okay. I'm taking care of her."

It was that last sentence that felt like a hot poker to the middle of my chest. "You're what? You're taking care of her?"

"Look, I just didn't want you to worry."

I'd been worried in such an intangible, unfocused way before. Now my concern had a shape. "Put her on the phone, Maria."

"She doesn't know I'm calling you. I should probably let you go." "N-n-no! Maria? Maria?"

She'd hung up. I had the number on my caller ID, but instead of calling her back, I dialed Olivia.

12. Sunday (Olivia)

I checked out of the hotel as soon as it was light out, the most depressing time to be in a casino. Everyone was slightly disheveled, hung over and scattered. Last night's nylons had torn or sagged at the ankles. Eye makeup had drifted lower on the face. Shirts were untucked with stains down the front. The pretty people who were there to have fun had gone to bed hours ago. The ones left playing slot machines in the wee hours of morning had a problem: addiction or lover's quarrel was my guess.

The parking garage was eerily quiet. I threw my suitcase in the back and climbed behind the wheel, hitting the automatic door lock as I pulled it closed. *Bang*. I put on my seatbelt and sat there for a few minutes, trying to get my breathing under control before starting out.

It hadn't been that hard to find her once I knew what I was looking for. After I'd gotten off the phone with my dad, I went back to the hotel and fired up my laptop. I ordered room service: a hamburger and fries, the frivolous expense justified by my unwillingness to talk to anyone. I dimmed the lights, but knew I wouldn't sleep. The television flashed muted infomercials as I imagined driving my rental car down a dusty road to the trailer park that was my mother's most recent address.

Three days after my eighteenth birthday, I answered the door to a woman on the front steps. It took me a few seconds to realize she was my mother.

I hadn't seen her in six years. She was thinner than I remembered, and older, obviously. She'd cut her hair short. She was fidgeting, her hands clasped in front of her while the fingers of one hand scratched the wrist of the other.

"We're not looking for a cleaning service," I said cruelly loud and deliberate as if I expected her to be unfamiliar with English.

"Olivia." She said it like she was calling my bluff, like she was disappointed in me for pretending not to know her.

I refused to be called out, to be scolded. I acted like I was refocusing on her face, recognizing her at last. "You don't belong here," I said, setting my jaw.

"Please, can we talk?"

I laughed then, a quick burst. It seemed so ridiculous. Did she expect to sit in the living room and have a chat?

"Charlotte could be home any minute." It wasn't true; Charlie was at Carmen's and wouldn't be home until after dinner, barring an emergency.

"I could take you up the street. We could talk over coffee?"

"I'm not going anywhere with you," I scoffed.

She flinched and nodded. "I want you to know how sorry I am."

I shrugged. I regretted my appearance: the sloppy ponytail, the pimple on my chin. I felt vaguely like I'd run into an ex-boyfriend not looking my best, missing the opportunity to make him kick himself for ditching me.

"How are you?" And when I said nothing: "And Charlotte. How's Charlotte?"

Charlie was twelve and struggling through seventh grade. She'd almost been held back last year; my dad had pleaded with the principal. If she and Carmen had to be separated, things would only get worse.

"The last thing she needs is to come home and find *you* here."

As I began to pull the door shut, my mother started to cry.

"Please!" she shouted.

"No," I barked back and the door clicked. I locked the bolt and listened as her sobs faded. I watched from the window as she sat in her car for several minutes. Her return suddenly seemed so inevitable, but the truth was that I'd never expected to see her again. If I ever thought of her, I imagined vaguely that she'd returned to her family in Mexico, the porous border fence acting improbably as a permanent wall between us. After the first few years, I'd stopped imagining it at all. I'd told so many people she was dead, for so long; it had begun to feel true.

But here she was, parked in a car in front of my house, crying messily and drawing attention to herself.

And she'd be back.

I left the front door hanging open and crossed the front yard in long strides. She startled when I knocked on her window, quickly wiping her face on her sleeve and rolling it down.

"I never want to see you here again."

"Olivia!"

"You have no right to do this to us. You left. We've gotten along fine without you and we don't want you back."

She started sobbing again.

"Leave us alone. Both of us. Especially Charlotte."

She covered her face, her shoulders shaking.

"Do you understand?"

She nodded and I went back in the house. When I looked out, hours later, her car was gone.

This time, it was my mother who came to the door surprised to see me.

I could just make out Charlie's figure, slumped on the couch behind her. When my mother said my name, Charlie sat up, her hands on her knees. It was darker inside than out; I couldn't make out her facial expression, but I was sure she could see mine.

My mother pushed open the screen, wordlessly, and, wordlessly, I stepped inside. Charlie and I stared at each other. She was wearing a dress I'd never seen before, blue floral that buttoned up the front. It was even stranger to see her this way, as if not even the smallest detail of this moment was one I could expect or understand.

When she continued to say nothing, I threw up my hands. "What the hell?" I shouted.

"Did you call her?" she asked, looking past me.

It made my stomach tighten to hear her talking *about me* to this woman, as if I wasn't even there.

My mother fidgeted, scratching at her arms. "I called your dad, Charlotte. Just to let him know you were okay."

"Wow." Charlie leaned back, casting her eyes away from both of us. "It only took three days for you to want to get rid of me this time," she mumbled.

"Charlotte, no." My mother stepped past me, closer to my sister. "I didn't even give him the address."

"Yeah well, thankfully there's an internet." I had a million questions, but it wasn't a conversation I wanted to have here. We could talk in the car. "Get your things. I'm taking you home."

Her head snapped up. "Who the hell do you think you are?" she hissed and I was taken aback, not understanding the level of hostility.

"Me?" I sputtered, stupidly. "What the hell is the matter with you?"

"If I wanted to talk to you, I would have called."

"Oh, really?" Like she was the queen of the universe and we all just served at her pleasure. "If you wanted to come see her, you could have told us."

"Oh, really?" she mimicked. "You would have *allowed* me to see my mother?"

I couldn't believe that after putting us through days of worry, she still felt entitled to be so rude. "We found your phone, we tracked down Isaac, dad got the police involved. He had to call the fucking *morgue."*

She flinched, but continued to look away.

My mother had wandered to the kitchen and seemed torn between giving us some space and getting involved.

"I'm not going back, Olivia, and you can't make me. I'm an adult."

"Why is it that I only ever hear that from you when you're having a tantrum? Don't tell me you're an adult: *act like one!"*

"I don't have to go, do I?" This, she shouted to my mother. I felt my authority slipping.

"You can't miss any more of your classes," I said, trying to keep the conversation between the two of us. My mother was hesitating. If I could just talk over any space, prevent her from jumping in, everything would be fine.

"Mom?"

Hearing that word from my sister's mouth made my breath catch in my throat.

My mother stepped toward us, one hand on the kitchen counter as if for balance. "Of course not, but—" She took a breath and let it out. "Is she right, Charlotte? About your classes?"

Charlie's face contorted with fury or betrayal, maybe both. She sprang to her feet and shoved past me, out the door. The screen slammed and as I moved to follow her, I felt my mother's hand on my shoulder.

"Let her go," she said.

I shook her off.

"She'll come back when she calms down."

"How do you know?" It was as if she thought the last five days made her an expert. A *Charlotte* whisperer.

"What other choice does she have?" she wondered quietly, almost to herself.

I watched out the screen as Charlie darted around the corner of the trailer next door.

"Can I get you a drink?" my mother asked.

"No." And then, as an afterthought: "Thank you."

"It's good to see you. I wish it was, obviously, better circumstances."

I nodded.

"Have a seat, Olivia. I need a cigarette." She grabbed her purse from the counter and seemed to throw herself out the door and down the steps.

I stood for a moment in the deserted living room, then pushed out the door after her.

I watched from behind as she fumbled with the lighter. It sputtered and flamed; she pulled in a breath so deep you'd think it was oxygen. "You have to smoke outside at your own house?" I asked.

"I don't want the furniture to stink. It makes quitting harder."

"Are you quitting?"

"Someday."

I sat on the step above the one she was sitting on. The sun was powerful, but there was enough of a breeze that I wasn't dying for conditioned air.

"What's with the dresses?" I asked.

"Church."

"Coming or going?"

"We were going." She looked at her watch and left the rest unsaid.

As I sat behind her, I couldn't see her face. She turned her head to the side as she exhaled and I caught glimpses of her profile. There was something undeniably graceful in the way her hand fluttered to her lips and then away, the cigarette between her slender fingers. She was like one of those old movie stars who made smoking look cool.

We settled into a long silence I found bearable. Then she dropped the cigarette and ground it out under her shoe. "Charlotte tells me you're a physical therapist?"

"Yes."

"Do you like it?"

I sighed. "Look, I don't want to be rude, but I didn't come here to talk to you."

She nodded.

At that moment, Charlie appeared, walking slowly. My mother got to her feet. "I'll take a walk." She headed toward Charlie, stopping to murmur something I couldn't hear. They hugged and parted. As Charlie got closer, I could tell she'd been crying.

She sat beside me with her arms across her chest.

"What's going on, Charlie? Why are you so angry?"

She slid away from me and turned, looking me straight in the eye. "You really don't know?"

I shook my head. Of course, it was dawning on me, but I'd need her to say it.

Charlie leaned toward me, narrowing her eyes. "She came back for us! And you sent her away!"

Ah, so there it was. It was my fault. I was chilled by the thought. How, after all these days, did it get to be my fault?

I looked away.

"Did you ever tell dad?" she asked.

My fault. I shrugged, seeing no value in withholding the truth. "I did not."

"Olivia! His wife returns and you don't think to mention it?"

"She didn't come back for him. She didn't even ask about him."

"But she asked about me."

"You were a child."

"A child without a mother."

I rolled my eyes, as if that was such a small thing. I didn't really think that, but she was trying to simplify something that wasn't simple.

Charlie leaned away, holding her arms so tightly, the flesh was white beneath her fingers.

"Well, it wasn't dad's fault," I said. "You can be mad at me all you want, but he didn't deserve to spend the week thinking you might be dead. And Carmen?"

"I emailed her."

"Oh, so that was you. She wasn't sure."

"Who else would it have been?"

"Charlie, we had no idea. Don't you understand?"

We sat quietly for a long moment. "I'll take the bus back tonight," she said. "I was planning on it anyway."

"So, I'm just supposed to leave you here? With her?"

"As opposed to, what? Dragging me home by my ear?"

The thought just made me tired. "Will you call dad?"

"Yes."

"Like, immediately. I will call him from the airport and he better have heard from you."

"Fine."

"I'm serious."

"Fine, Olivia!" She stood up. "Just go!"

It actually came as a relief. In moments, I would be in the cool, quiet of my rental car, leaving this behind me. She was alive and her anger was all my fault and I just wanted to be *away*. "Do you need money?"

She shook her head, her lips pressed tight. She could use her credit card now, so she could afford a principled stance.

In one of my earliest memories, I'm stamping my tiny feet as my mother fills a pot at the sink. She's imploring me to *stop whining*. But I don't. And she throws the pot of water over my head and runs crying from the room.

By the time Charlotte was born, I was well acquainted with my mother's intolerance for whining. I'd come home from school and she'd hand the baby to me and go into her bedroom to take a nap. I remember trying to quiet Charlie's cries by tapping my hand over the tiny O of her mouth, creating a warrior call that – when I was lucky –made her laugh. She'd nap in her car seat on my bedroom floor, as far away from my sleeping mother as possible. I'd do my homework while steadily rocking the seat with my foot.

When my dad finally came home from work, my mother would be showered and dressed, getting dinner ready. She'd often greet him at the door with Charlotte perched happily on her hip.

Charlie was never as concerned about my mother's moods as I was. She was a tantrum-prone toddler, a whiney kindergartener. She was full of energy, couldn't sit still, and only had one volume: loud. It didn't seem logical to me. Being quiet was about self-preservation. My mother's slaps stung; her sharp nails left half-moon indents on fleshy upper-arms. I did what I could to be the buffer between the two of them. But they were alone during the day while I was at school.

After my mother left, I wondered if it was because Charlie was so much more difficult than I was. It was unfair to blame my young sister for such a thing, and I never said it out loud, but I thought it.

I spoke to my father from the airport. Charlie had called him and as relieved as he sounded about that, there was a new kind of tension in his voice. He didn't like that I'd left her behind, but he didn't seem to have any other ideas.

The flight was short, but still long enough to go over my conversation with Charlie a few thousand times. I'd said all the wrong things. Or, to be more accurate, I hadn't said the thing I should have said, which was this: she was right.

She'd been a child when my mother came to see me; that was true. But she wasn't a child anymore and I'd had no right to keep it from her.

My father met me at the airport, but he didn't get out of the car. I threw my bag into the backseat and climbed into the passenger's side. He patted my arm in lieu of a hug and navigated into the traffic.

"Where am I taking you?"

"My place. I need to face Oscar sooner or later. I'll pick up Charlie at the bus station. It'll be the middle of the night. There's no sense both of us staying up."

"I'll be up," he snapped.

"Okay." I watched the muscle in his jaw pulsate. "Dad?"

"Charlie says your mother came to the house several years ago and you kept that to yourself."

The truth was, it had never occurred to me to mention it. I told no one about her visit, which made it easier to pretend it hadn't happened. "Yes," I said.

"Your sister's very upset. Where did you get the idea that it was your place to make that decision?"

Without meaning to, I let out a short bark of laughter. "Where did I get the idea? Are you serious? Dad, I love you, but you put me in that place. I raised that girl just as much as you."

He began shaking his head, wildly, scowling. "You helped, certainly. And I'm grateful, but—"

"No, dad, *you* helped." I was gripping the door handle, adrenaline burning in the center of my chest. "You paid rent, bought groceries, came home every night. But I made the important decisions. I was the parent."

Neither of us spoke for the rest of the ride. When he dropped me off in front of my apartment, he said: "I'll pick up your sister."

In the middle of the night, I woke to the ringing of my home phone. No one ever called that number besides telemarketers and my father. Oscar was sleeping on top of my feet, a conditional forgiveness based on my not moving. After a fitful night of sleep at the hotel, I'd collapsed in bed shortly after crossing the threshold. I reached for the receiver, imagining an apology. Instead, he sounded irate.

Charlie had never gotten off the bus.

13. Monday (Charlie)

"Charlotte! Charlotte, wake up!"

I rub my face, trying to remember where I am.

"I have half a dozen messages from your father. Did you tell him you were taking the bus last night?"

I squint in the early morning light. My mother's face looms close and I'm startled to recognize: she's angry.

I sit up. "I left a message for Olivia. I told her."

She narrows her eyes at me. I see her trying to determine if she can trust me. She sighs and I'm not sure what she's decided. "He's frantic. You need to call him." She puts her cell phone in my hand. "Now."

He answers on the first ring. I explain that my mother turns her phone off while she sleeps; we only just got his messages. Yes, I'm still in Vegas. I decided to fly back today rather than take the bus. It's faster and only a little bit more money. I'll be well-rested and back in time for my class at 3:00. Carmen has agreed to pick me up at the airport. I got Olivia's voicemail when I called yesterday and assumed she'd turned it off for the flight. I don't know why she didn't pass my message along.

I was surprised when Olivia agreed to leave so quickly yesterday. It wasn't until my mother returned, so obviously disappointed, that I understood. She'd been hoping to spend more time with Olivia. The feeling wasn't mutual.

When I get off the phone with my dad, I feel another wave of shame. He'd had no idea about my mother's visit all those years ago and I'd punished him anyway. Olivia said he'd called the morgue. And now, accidentally, I'd done it again. I picture him waiting for me to get off a bus in the middle of the night.

I skip breakfast, my stomach in guilty knots. My mother and I barely speak on the drive to the airport, the early morning hour excusing our silence. When she pulls up to the curbside drop-off, I turn to say my goodbyes, but she's turned away, opening her door. I get out and meet her on the sidewalk.

She smiles brightly and opens her arms for a hug, but I hesitate. Warm air rushes around us, a mix of exhaust and departing cars and what passes for a breeze in Nevada. A bus horn blares.

"Will I see you again?" I ask, the pitch of my voice higher than I want it to be.

"Of course you will." She laughs, surprised.

"When?"

She stammers then and I feel motion sick, my stomach dropping like it does on an unexpected hill. Rollercoaster Road between my house and Carmen's.

I pull my backpack off the ground and step back as I struggle with the straps. She reaches for me, her grip tight on the bare skin of my arm; she pulls me close and forces me to meet her eyes. "Anytime, Charlotte. Just call me. I'm not far."

I should just leave it there – hug her and go catch my plane – but I don't.

"My birthday is Sunday," I say.

She scowls. "I know when your birthday is."

"Will you come?"

Her face gives too much away. She tries to cover. "Won't you have family obligations?"

"You're family."

She smiles but it's a defeated smile like by me winning, she has lost. She looks away. "I'm not sure your dad would want me—"

"I'll talk to him."

She strokes my arm, nodding. "Okay. Talk to your dad."

"And you'll come?"

"I'll ask for the time off when I go in today."

Satisfied, I hug her goodbye.

Carmen is wearing dark sunglasses that cover most of her elfin face. I slide into the car beside her and set my bag on the floor. She forgave me over the phone, but I'm relieved to feel her forgiveness in the strength of her embrace. She only lets me go when a car behind us beeps, wanting our spot.

She turns her head and sniffs, but I can't see her eyes. "So, what's she like?" she asks. The car pulls away from the curb and we're off. "Tell me everything."

And I do. I tell her about how beautiful my mother is, how you'd never guess she was in her forties. And a smoker. I tell her how my mother sits on her front steps blowing smoke rings into the night air. I tell her about Ben and the embarrassing truth that I'd thought he was flirting with me when really he's just totally in love with her. How obvious it is when he talks about her and how proud he is of her recovery. I tell her about the night we tried on dresses and she told me that leaving me was the biggest regret of her life. I tell her everything.

She listens while I talk, nodding her head, changing lanes on the interstate. Once the car settles to a comfortable temperature, I lower the fan on the air conditioner.

"And she's coming to my birthday on Sunday so you'll get to meet her," I say as we pull into the lot at Pima.

She groans and I'm not sure what this signals. It's the first noise she's made since we left the airport. I press my lips into a straight line and wait.

"I'm not going to be around this weekend," she says.

"What?" It comes out like an accusation; I can't help it.

Carmen pulls the car into a spot at the back even though there are empty spots closer. "Things have been getting pretty bad with me lately." She says this to the steering wheel.

"What do you mean?"

"Food-wise," she says and she removes her sunglasses. I notice that her features are a bit sharper than normal. She turns toward me, pressing her back to the door and pulling a leg under her. She's wearing skinny jeans and I think how appropriate that is; it seems they were designed specifically for the starving.

I take a breath, steeling myself for the rest. While I've been away, wrapped up in my own drama, Carmen has been battling her demons by herself. She'd gone to the emergency room with a racing heartbeat; blood tests revealed her electrolytes were out of whack. Scared, she'd confided enough of the details to her parents for them to arrange for her to go to a treatment center. They'd wanted her to go today, but she'd refused.

"I had to see you first," she says.

I take her hands in mine, squeezing the delicate long fingers. "I'm so sorry I wasn't here."

"It's not your fault. I've been headed this way for awhile."

I nod, appreciating the kindness of her lie. "When do you leave?"

"Tomorrow." She cringes. "I'll miss your birthday."

"God, don't worry about that."

"And meeting your mom!"

"You'll meet her another time."

She nods and only then starts to cry. “I was so worried when you were gone. Don’t ever do that to me again.”

I start crying then too. “I won’t,” I say and she lets me hold her as sobs wrack her tiny body.

“I don’t know what I’d do without you. I just don’t.”

Neither do I.

Carmen goes home to pack and I go to class. I’ve been gone for a week and I need to catch up. Luckily, there’s always an organized good student willing to email notes in exchange for friendly conversation and gratitude. In this class, it’s Sadie Wilkins. She’s easy to spot, always getting to class early, sitting in the front, taking notes on her laptop. She wears her curly, dark hair in a high ponytail and always remembers to bring a sweater for the air conditioner. I give a vague excuse, something about a “personal problem” and Sadie nods and tells me not to worry.

Our professor dims the lights and shows a video about a malnourished pit bull that’s rescued, fattened up, and then put to sleep because his food aggression prevents him from being adoptable. It doesn’t seem fair. If you spend the first years of your life being starved, you should be allowed to be territorial about your food dish. The world should cut you a break. We all have baggage.

Whenever professors show videos, I assume they’re hung over.

Carmen had gone to Pima because that’s where I was going. She didn’t have to go to community college. She got A’s all through high school and kicked ass at her SAT’s. She’d gotten into the University of Arizona and never told her parents. I found the acceptance letter on her nightstand, tucked under a pile of other things, the familiar emblem across the top of the letterhead.

I held it out to her and she shook her head, refusing to even touch it.

“I can’t go without you,” she said and I knew just how she felt. I was surprised, though, because I’d always thought it was me needing her through school.

I didn’t encourage her to go to school without me. Whenever I considered how selfish that made me, I told myself that I’d saved her from a lifetime of student loan debt.

After class, my dad is waiting for me. He's sitting on a park bench and when he sees me, he jumps to his feet and heads over. He can't even wait for me to go to him. It would be cute if it weren't so embarrassing. Or maybe it's the other way around.

I break off from the group of students I've been walking with and my dad grabs hold of me with an enthusiasm he hasn't allowed himself since I was a kid. He hugs me tightly; my face is pressed into his shoulder. I lift my head, tucking my chin against his collar.

"I'm sorry," I say.

"I know, I know," he says and he pounds me on the back, then puts his arm around me and walks me toward his car.

Once we're driving, he starts asking about Carmen. He's spoken to her parents this morning which means he knew before I did. Carmen's eating disorder has always been vaguely understood by the adults in our life, but the true severity was usually withheld. If I'm honest with myself, it was sometimes withheld from me. Only Carmen ever knows how bad it really is.

"It's a great facility," my dad says. "I think it's popular with celebrities. Anyway, they'll take care of her."

The rehab center is in Wickenburg, a few hours north of Tucson. I looked it up online once, though I never told Carmen. It resembles a resort and they even have horses. Carmen's parents must have good insurance. "Maybe she'll make friends with a Disney starlet." I try to sound upbeat.

He turns on the radio and invites me to choose a station. I lean forward and press the "seek" button. When it's gone around twice, I switch it off. Too many commercials.

"Did your sister ever apologize?" he asks.

"Not exactly."

He grunts as he flips on his blinker and slides into the middle lane. The light is turning from yellow to red. His brakes squeak.

"And your mother?"

My breath catches in my throat at the unfamiliar words. I hadn't known how we'd talk about her. "And my mother, what?"

The light turns green and he takes the turn, clears his throat. "Did she apologize?"

"Yes."

"Well, that's something."

There's a long silence between us and I'm afraid this will be the end of it. The last week will be forgotten as though it never happened and we'll go back to the unspoken agreement to never talk about my mother. I feel the door swinging shut.

"I invited her to my birthday party," I say, sticking my foot in the metaphorical threshold, keeping it open.

He clears his throat again, this time louder and longer than the first. "Did you?" he says, finally, and I don't answer. "That should be interesting." He shakes his head and laughs, reaching over to pat my knee so I know he isn't mad.

14. Tuesday (Olivia)

My second patient of the day was late so when my third patient came in, we were already running over his appointment time. It felt hectic and overbooked for the second day that week and I was grateful for the distraction. I handed him off to a trainee at the Pilates machine and met Sara in the waiting room.

"When I saw your name on my schedule, I wasn't sure it was real," I told her.

Sara grinned up at me from her wheelchair. She had dirty-blond hair and rectangular glasses. "Oh, it's real. It only took, what, five months?"

Her insurance stopped covering her in November. Her diagnosis was progressive, but they didn't have the terminology for a medical condition that didn't get better. Not getting worse wasn't just the goal; it was fantastic. We'd both been writing letters to her insurance company as part of their appeals process.

I pointed her to my cubicle and walked behind her as she rolled forward. "Posture still looking good," I said. Before she'd started seeing me, her right shoulder rolled forward. I'd made her a harness out of a therapy band twisted into a figure eight. She'd only worn it for a week before she was able to correct it on her own, unconsciously. I stood in front of the computer and opened her file. "Have you noticed any changes to your abilities since I saw you last?"

She grimaced. "It's hard to tell from one day to the next because it's so slow, but I think my legs aren't as strong as they were five months ago. And sometimes I get that shoulder pain like I used to."

"How are your transfers?"

She paused as if she had to think it over. "Harder," she admitted, finally.

"Falls?"

"No."

"Good." Before the insurance had lapsed, we recreated a hypothetical fall scenario in the bathroom and she was able to pull herself up to the toilet, using the grab bars. She was wiped out by the time she went home that day, but it was a success.

It was crazy for Medicaid to deny her. If she stopped being strong enough to live independently, the government would be on the hook for a lot more care. It was in everyone's best interest that she keep her strength up.

"How did you do on your home exercise program?" I asked. We'd made a list on her last day, naming them things she'd remember. There was marching, punching, shoulder pinches, butt clenches, rowing, ankle alphabets, clams. I sent her home with a list of twenty-one exercises.

She made another face. "I'm awful without someone to check in with."

Accountability. I understood. "Let's get back on track." I decided to spend the fifty minutes working on the mats. She put her arms around my neck and I lifted her to standing position, pivoted, and lowered her to the floor. The first time we'd done this, she didn't trust me.

"But you're so little," she'd said skeptically, and whimpered the whole time I did the lift. After the first few, she stopped whimpering.

Sara was taller than me, something that only became noticeable after I got her standing, but she didn't weigh more than a hundred pounds. Her arms were buff, though. All that wheeling around.

Sara rolled onto her stomach and got onto her hands and knees. She lifted one arm, then switched and lifted the other, maintaining her balance. I held her shoulders from behind as she raised up into a high kneel, then a "Captain Morgan" pose. She pulled herself to her feet, gripping the edge of the exam table. I directed her to bend her knees, shifting right to left, over and over as I stood behind her, holding her hips.

She was out of breath when she left and I felt satisfied.

Before I finished for the day, I wrote a stellar eval. No way they'd deny coverage again.

I found Greg waiting on the sidewalk as I was leaving.

"What you reading?"

He closed the book, using his finger to mark the page, and tilted the cover toward me. 1984. "It's a reread."

"Does it feel like you're reading about the present?"

He laughed. "Nah. It's definitely a sobering warning, though."

I nod. I'd read the book in high school. It had regained popularity in recent years as discussions of the surveillance state dominated the news.

"How was your weekend?"

I rolled my eyes. "Well, I went to Vegas like you suggested."

He raised his eyebrows. "And?"

"I found her. She's home now."

"That's great. What—" He hesitates, politely.

"It's just a long story." I sighed. "Wanna get a beer?"

"I got nowhere I gotta be," he said with a smile.

"Are you sure I'm not boring you?" I asked again as the waitress left us with our laminated menus. We'd chosen a table outside; in the shade of the awning, the air felt pleasant, almost cool.

"Of course not. Go on."

In the car, I'd already explained the background: the maternal abandonment. "It seems so obvious now, but it really hadn't occurred to me that Charlie would go looking for her. She never even asked about her as a kid." I saw this differently now, of course. Charlie never asked about our mother because she'd picked up the lesson my father and I taught her with our silence.

"So you saw her?"

"My mother? Yeah."

"What was that like?"

Looking at Greg across the table, platitudes deserted me. "It was so hard."

"Mmm." Somehow, he managed to convey a sense of solidarity with a murmur.

"My father left after I was diagnosed. Parents aren't supposed to be weak. It's hard to forgive."

"I'm not a big believer in forgiveness when it comes to that sort of thing."

"I don't really think forgiveness is about the other person." Greg brushed his dark hair off his forehead. "It's about letting go of the anger. For you. I have no idea where my father is and I don't care. But I don't go to sleep praying for his torment. I'm not invested in it."

"I buy that. Until Sunday, I'd hardly spent any time thinking about my mother."

"And when you saw her?"

"Hm. Yeah, the anger came back, I guess. I felt like her existence diminished me somehow. Like I was reduced to competing with her."

"Competing?"

"For Charlie." I shook my head to rid myself of the memory. "I know she's supposed to be all grown up, but it still feels like she's mine."

"Like you're her mother?"

"No. Not her mother. Just—" I struggled to find words. "The thing she got instead of a mother. I am that thing because my mother left. And if she comes back, I stop being that thing." I shrugged. "I don't know if that makes sense."

"I think so. But maybe you don't have to stop being that thing regardless of who your mother is being."

I mulled that over while the waitress took our order. We got nachos to go with our beers. The outdoor patio faced the parking lot so I watched the familiar blue truck claim its spot before the owner got out and walked closer, smiling with surprised recognition when he saw me.

I did the introductions – Rick: Greg, Greg: Rick – and was dismayed when Rick decided to sit with us until his buddies arrived. He hadn't been invited, but that didn't seem to dawn on him.

When Greg asked how we knew each other, I said we'd met in college. It was technically true; I don't know why I didn't just tell the truth. But what was the truth? Ex-boyfriend? Friend? Recent fuck-buddy, but never again and this time I mean it? His identity was in flux.

Rick just rolled his eyes at me. "Yeah. We've known each other forever. How about you?"

"We met at work," I said.

Rick noticed Greg's wheelchair then and made a big show of it, leaning back in his chair. "Are you one of her patients?"

I shook my head, embarrassed. It made me uncomfortable, this collision of worlds.

"No, we just met outside the office. I'm sure she'd never have let me chat her up if I was her patient."

The waitress came to the table then and the phrase "chat her up" rang in my ears as she set down our drinks and asked if Rick was ordering. He explained that he was keeping us company while he waited for his party, but he'd have a Dos Equis when she got a minute. She wandered off again, leaving us alone.

"What'd you get?" Rick lifted my beer right out of my hand and took a territorial sip. "Not bad," he said and he turned the bottle, reading the label.

There was an awkward silence. What could the three of us discuss, besides the weather? I wracked my brain for some common ground. "So I found Charlie. She's home."

"Oh, see? I told you." And then to Greg: "I told her."

The waitress came by with Rick's beer.

"So where was she?"

This didn't work. Now Rick and I were in a conversation that excluded Greg. "It's a lot to get into and your friends will be here soon."

"But she's fine?"

I nodded. "Seems to be warming up faster than usual." I said it out of sheer desperation and felt truly grateful when Greg picked up the thread and began going on about how he tried not to complain about the heat; after years of whining over Midwestern winters, it felt hypocritical.

Greg and Rick exchanged some banter on global warming. I looked at my watch. Where were Rick's friends?

Rick shifted in his seat, facing Greg. "Well, I've got a lot of respect for you."

"For me?" Greg looked confused and I had a sinking feeling I knew where this conversation was headed.

Rick nodded. "I don't think I could do it," he said, gesturing toward Greg's wheelchair. "If that happened to me. I don't know if I'd be able to live."

Greg looked away, noticeably uncomfortable.

"You'd live," I said, flatly, trying to figure out a smooth way to change the subject, now that I'd already used up Charlie and the weather.

"Really, though." Rick was shaking his head. "All the things I'd never be able to do again. The loss of freedom." If he wasn't on his first beer, I might have been less disgusted with him.

"You find other things." Greg took a swig of his beer and looked away, as if willing his body to follow his gaze.

Rick wouldn't shut up. "I don't know, man. I think you're pretty fuckin' great."

Greg sighed and leaned forward, elbows on the table. "I know you think you're complimenting me, but you're basically telling me you think my life is so depressing, I should want to die."

"No, no, no. I just don't think I have what it takes, you know? You're just so positive, man. It's awesome to see." Rick held up his beer bottle.

"Yeah, okay." Greg clinked bottles and looked at me. "I'm a fuckin' inspiration."

I shrugged and tried to apologize for Rick with my face. "I guess so."

Mercifully, three of Rick's buddies approached the table and Rick got to his feet, said goodbye, and drifted inside to the bar in a cloud of raucous laughter.

I turned back to Greg. He held his beer bottle up to me. "For having the bravery to get up in the morning and make it through the whole day without offing myself." He was smiling, but his eyes suggested another emotion.

I lifted my beer bottle, but set it down again without clinking. "I'm so sorry."

He shrugged. "It's okay. I'm used to it."

"Well, that sucks."

He laughed. We finished the nachos and talked more about our parents. Greg's mother still lived in Ohio, but came out to visit every Christmas with his sister and seemed to be trying to figure out a way to convince her to apply to graduate school in Arizona.

"She'd probably already have moved here if it weren't for my sister. Now it's like Sophie's Choice."

"She didn't want you to move away."

"She understood. She just wants the family together. It's like, a biological urge."

I pulled a chip from the dwindling pile. "I think I'm in a fight with my dad."

"You think?"

"The last time we talked, I said some stuff I shouldn't have. We didn't leave it in a good place. I've never really been in a fight with my dad before. I'm not really sure how to fix it."

"Well, maybe just tell him you're sorry?"

When the check came, neither of us had cash and I argued that he should let me get it since I'd eaten more of the nachos. He protested, but relented.

"Only if you let me get it next time."

I smiled. "Fair enough," I said and I wrote my number on a paper napkin.

After I dropped Greg back at his apartment, I decided to take his advice. The last time I'd talked to my father was Monday morning, after he'd heard from Charlie in Vegas and confirmed that she'd decided to fly back instead of taking the bus. I'd missed Charlie's message because I'd turned my cell phone off for the flight and fell asleep in my apartment before remembering to turn it back on. My father texted me later that day to let me know she'd arrived, but I still hadn't seen her since leaving her in Nevada.

I was relieved that Charlie's car wasn't in the driveway. One apology at a time. I tried to shake off the feeling that it wasn't fair, that after the events of the past week, I was the one who was in the doghouse. I hadn't abandoned my children or run away from home. Whatever. It was what it was.

I let myself in the front door and found my dad on the couch. He muted the television but did not get up.

"Hey." I set my keys on the table by the door and sat in the chair across from him. It was his "man" chair, a cushy recliner we'd gotten him for Father's Day a few years ago. He only ever sat in it for our benefit, to be polite. I'd never found him sitting there on his own.

"Hey."

Charlie had never paid her half of that chair. Whenever we went in on a gift together, it usually meant she picked it out and I paid.

"Where's Charlie?"

My dad sat forward. "She's at Carmen's. They're having a… situation."

"Situation?"

"Carmen's going to a treatment center for her eating disorder. She leaves today."

I tried to remember the last time I'd seen her, while I was grilling her about Charlie. She hadn't seemed any thinner than she normally did. "I knew she had a problem, but I didn't know it was that bad."

"I guess so."

"Wow. Do you know how long she'll be there?"

"Not really. I think it depends. I spoke to Lydia very briefly. She was pretty broken up."

I could only imagine. "How's Charlie taking it?"

"Hard to say. I think she's got her guard up or maybe it just hasn't sunk in yet." He shrugged. "She's keeping it together so far. She's over there now so she can see Carmen off."

"Poor kid," I said, meaning Carmen. "Though when you look at the big picture, it's probably a good thing that she's getting help."

"Probably so." But he shook his head. "Ironic, though."

"How do you mean?"

"Lydia and Jorge are such good parents. And they end up with a kid in rehab."

"Well, I guess parenting is just one factor. There are all these… intangibles."

"Hmm." He rubbed his chin and I could hear the scratch of fingernails on his nearly invisible evening stubble. "And yet you girls grow up orphans and look at you."

"Dad, we were hardly orphans." I scowled at him. Silence swelled between us and I took a breath. Why was it so hard? "About what I said the other day—"

He waved me off. "You were right. I left you on your own too much. Both of you."

"No you didn't."

"I expected you to be the other parent."

I sighed. "Sometimes. But you did your best."

He shrugged and got to his feet then, my near-apology seeming to make us equally uncomfortable, and I followed him into the kitchen. "Want a milkshake?" he asked.

Growing up, my dad made the best milkshakes. He would claim they were for special occasion, but he made the occasions up. We had milkshakes to celebrate the end of the week, the first sighting of an ocotillo in bloom, the fact that we were all wearing the same color shirt.

"What's the occasion?"

He pulled the blender out of the upper cabinet. He spent so long setting it up, untangling the electric cord that I wasn't sure he planned on answering. "Because it could be worse," he said, finally, and he pulled the ice cream out of the freezer.

15. Wednesday (Charlie)

It's my job to talk to Dan, Carmen's boyfriend. She hadn't even told him she was leaving. Yesterday, when I asked how much he knew about her eating stuff, she just shrugged. "He's seen me naked. Sort of."

I assumed that meant they did it with the lights out, but before I could get clarification, Carmen's mother knocked on the bedroom door and told us it was time to go.

I'd like someone to blame, but it won't be Dan. Carmen's eating problems precede this boyfriend or even the hypothetical boyfriends of adolescence. In high school, Carmen had dated the same boy since we were sophomores. They lost their virginity to each other a whole year before I managed to lose mine. I hated that year; she felt so far away. When we talked, there was a new air of "you don't understand" weighing down every interaction. Things didn't really go back to normal until Mateo went away to college and she seemed to remember that boys would come and go; our friendship was forever.

She'd been dating Dan for six months. Having survived her first love and first heartbreak, she'd emerged much more practical and less romantic. They'd met in her Psychology of Human Sexuality class and they'd been eager to try out all the positions in the textbook. Apparently, he was an overachiever in the bedroom, but as far as I could tell, it ended there. He was too quiet in social settings to be sure he was dumb, but that was the feeling I got.

After my morning class, I find Dan standing outside in a group of guys, wearing a sleeveless athletic jersey with a number on it. I know so little about sports that I don't even know which one it's for, let alone what team.

He smiles and says my name as I approach.

"Can I talk to you for a minute?"

His face falls and he rubs the top of his shaved head. He punches one of his buddies on the arm, a Neanderthal's goodbye, and follows me to a picnic table.

We sit across from each other. "Carmen asked me to talk to you."

He says nothing, just licks his lips. He looks so nervous and it dawns on me that he thinks she's sent me to break up with him.

"She's had to go to the hospital."

His face flashes quickly with a look that can only be relief. Then his eyes widen. "The hospital?"

"Well, more of a treatment center," I say. "For eating disorders."

He blinks.

"Did you know?"

He shakes his head. "She used to do these weird things like, scrape the cheese off her pizza. When she told me she was afraid of the fat, I'd just tell her she was crazy. But, to be honest, I kinda thought all girls were like that."

Interestingly, I kind of think so too. It was all about degrees. What woman could say she hadn't denied herself food when she was hungry? When does that cross the line into a disorder? Sometimes, that answer is obvious; Carmen crossed that line a long time ago. But what about the skinny girl who refuses dessert? The one who responds to her freshman fifteen by eating celery all summer? What about all those women trading cleanse recipes on Facebook?

He puts his elbows on the table and buries his face in his big hands. "How could I not know?" His voice cracks and I'm startled. Is he going to cry?

"It's been like this since we were kids," I explain. "She's gotten pretty good at hiding it."

He rubs his head again and looks across the table at me. "How long will she be gone?"

"Sometimes thirty days, but they do an assessment when she arrives. She just got there last night." She left the house with her dad. He drove her to the clinic and I stayed behind with her mom who didn't want to fall apart in front of the doctors. Mrs.Rodriguez maintained her brave face until we heard the garage door close. Then she cried and, not knowing what to say, I held her hand.

"Can we talk to her? Can we visit?"

These are the right questions. I'm wondering if I misjudged him and so I find myself inviting him to my birthday party. He would have tagged along with Carmen anyway. Her parents will be there. It'll be good for us to stick together and support each other while she's gone.

I run into Isaac in the parking lot. I'd slipped into Ethics late yesterday, sat in the back, and was able to beat him to the exit. The mass of students filling the hall between us allowed me to avoid him.

Assuming he was even trying to catch up.

He's leaning against my car, eyeing me as I approach.

I unlock the door without saying anything.

"You're just going to ignore me?"

"Trying." I yank the door open and throw my backpack inside.

He puts a hand on my shoulder and I shake him off, wheeling around to face him.

"Are you going to tell me what happened?" he asks.

"You think you're entitled to an explanation?" As he pauses to mull that over, I get into the driver's seat and pull the door shut.

"Are we broken up?" I start the engine and I hear his voice muffled through the closed window.

I roll it down. "Are you kidding? You're kidding."

He doesn't answer. I drive away.

I've worked at my father's office since I was sixteen. Mostly, I answer the phones while I do my homework, sign people in at the front desk. Dentist's offices are the quietest places, better than study hall. None of my dad's patients pass salacious notes or make farting noises and collapse into fits of laughter.

There's no one behind the desk when I enter. There are two older women in the waiting room, sitting four seats apart and consumed by different issues of Good Housekeeping. I open the door to the reception area and find Mrs. Carver crouched down in front of a filing cabinet. She looks up, startled, as if she's been caught doing something illicit. When she sees it's just me, she starts laughing.

"Oh dear, you caught me swearing my head off at whoever does the filing here." She slams the drawer shut and stands up, pulling her beige skirt down to cover her ample thighs. "Unfortunately, that's me."

"I didn't hear a thing," I assure her, sliding my backpack off my shoulder.

When I was younger, Olivia had worked here and somehow made it look so glamorous. In the summer, I'd have to stay in my dad's office while the grown ups worked, surrounded by all those shelves full of unreadable books. Olivia got to wear slight heels with her work outfit and I could hear the clickety-clack of her footsteps up and down the halls.

By the time I started working here, Olivia had gone to college. Mrs. Carver was sweet, but she wore orthopedic shoes and the gossip she had access to was much less fascinating.

She hugs me now, which is not our custom, but she doesn't mention my week away.

"You reading anything good?"

"Not this semester."

All through high school, she'd read my assigned reading along with me. It started when she realized my father was doing this, always had, so we could talk about it and he could help me with my papers. I knew he'd never done this with Olivia, because she'd never struggled in school, but it didn't offend me. I liked having this connection with him, the special attention.

When Mrs. Carver joined our reading group, I was reading things like The House of Seven Gables and The Count of Monte Cristo. She'd complain that my teachers seemed to think that nothing of value had been written by a woman, or in the last fifty years.

"They don't make vet techs read the classics?" she teases.

I sit at the desk and begin removing the large textbooks from my backpack. She cringes.

"You looking forward to the end of the semester?" Mrs. Carver sits at the other desk, placing a stack of folders in front of her.

I shrug. "It's hard to look forward to when I know finals come first." This semester will be especially hard, without Carmen. Even though we don't have the same classes anymore, haven't since we were freshmen, we'd still study together. Mostly I look forward to summer because Carmen will be back. Without her, I have no one to really talk to.

A door opens. My father shakes hands with an old man in the hallway and heads to his office. The old man starts toward the desk to check out, make a follow-up appointment.

I turn to Mrs. Carver. "I want to talk to my dad."

She closes the folder and shimmies her rolling chair toward me, Flintstone's style. "Sure, honey. I got this. You go ahead."

I get to my feet and walk slowly down the hall. Behind me, Mrs. Carver pitches her voice higher and asks to be of service. My father has left the door to his office slightly open and I tap my fingernails lightly across the wood.

"Come in." He's sitting behind the desk. His white coat is hanging on the hook just inside the door.

"How come you never wear your coat inside this office?"

He shrugs. "I don't know. Habit?" He reaches for some M&M's in a dish and pops them in his mouth. He slides the dish closer to me.

I shake my head and sit in the chair in front of his desk. I slouch.

"What's new?"

"Been thinking."

"'Bout what?"

"Did you know she was an alcoholic?"

He steeples his hands on the desktop and is quiet, but he doesn't pretend not to know who I'm talking about, who she is. "News to me," he says, finally. "But then, most things are, when it comes to her." He shakes his head. "I missed a lot." His steepled hands collapse under his focused attention.

It's unkind, I realize, to push him for answers he's probably wracked his brain over for years.

"She's not still drinking," he says suddenly, as if the idea has startled him from his reverie.

"No, she's sober."

He nods. In the silence, I wonder what he was going to say if I'd answered differently.

I sit cross-legged in the middle of my unmade bed with my laptop on my knees. There's nothing more useless than making a bed. If the Queen of England comes to visit, I'll throw the bedspread over the rumpled sheets. The house rule is that as long as it doesn't spill into the rest of the house, I can be as messy in my own room as I want. I just have to keep the door closed. Both things are fine by me.

I scroll through my Facebook page. Isaac and I were never "Facebook official" which simplifies things, but a part of me longs for that kind of public severing of ties. *Charlotte Howard has changed her romantic status to single.* I try to think of a passive aggressive status update, but everything I come up with is redundant and petty and makes me miss Carmen. She'd help me think of something really great, then talk me out of posting it.

Sometimes we're good for each other.

I start typing into the search bar: U of A transfer application.

There's a quick knock and I close the lid on my laptop as Olivia pushes the door open. "Hey."

"Hey."

I don't ask her to come inside. She leans in the doorway. "I heard about Carmen. Are you okay?"

"Yeah. It's a good thing. A long time coming." I slide my computer onto the bed and press my back against the pillows at the headboard. I hug my knees to my chest.

"It is a good thing," she says a little too loud. "She's really brave to admit that she needs help."

"I know."

She looks at the carpet for a long moment, then takes a breath and steps into the room like it's a dare she's given herself. She pushes the door shut behind her as she moves forward. "We were going to have a big party, a cookout, for your birthday this weekend. But we could postpone it 'til after she gets back. Do something small?" She perches on the foot of the bed. She's somehow both near and far, closer than she has a right to be while still maintaining a safe distance.

"No. I want to have it," I say.

"You do?"

"I invited someone." My voice cracks and I try to cover by coughing. The rest I say in a much deeper voice, in a rush: "Mom. I invited Mom."

Olivia's eyebrows lift and she looks out the window. She just sits there breathing, like just that takes a lot of effort.

"Does dad know?" she asks.

"Mmhm."

She takes that in without shifting her gaze. "I don't understand how you can forgive her so easily," she says softly.

"There's nothing easy about it."

She's quiet, nodding like she understands, but I'm sure she doesn't.

"Did you ever wonder why she left?" I ask.

"Does it matter?"

"Of course it matters."

She shrugs. "It doesn't matter to me."

"She's an alcoholic."

She looks at me blankly.

"She's in recovery now but she was drunk most of the time she was gone."

"So what? So she left us because she was drinking?"

I realize suddenly that my mother never actually said this. She didn't describe it in such detail. I hesitate. "You don't think that makes a difference?" I choose my words carefully.

"Not to me."

"How can you say that? Alcoholism is a disease."

Olivia rolls her eyes.

"You said Carmen was brave for going to rehab. What's the difference?"

"Well, for one thing, Carmen never abandoned her children. She never abandoned me."

"That's a pretty self-centered view of forgiveness. It's only for people who haven't hurt you?"

"Or my baby sister."

"Look, don't pretend you're staying mad at her on my account."

"I'm not mad. I just don't feel the need to invite her to my birthday parties."

"Well, I do," I say. "I want a relationship with my mother and you don't get to decide whether I can have one."

"Fine."

We're quiet. I cross my legs underneath me again and lean forward, my hands on my thighs. "You criticize my forgiving nature, while you hope to benefit from it."

"What does that mean?"

"Hell, you don't even bother to apologize. Like it's nothing."

"Like what's nothing?"

"Keeping my mother from me!"

She looks away and rubs her forehead with the tips of her fingers. "You know what? If you want a relationship with her, that's your business."

I cross my arms at her. "It is my business."

"Just like it's my business if I don't want a relationship with her."

I shrug. "Fine."

She stands.

"Well, she's gonna be here on Sunday."

"Great." She walks to the door and turns back, her hand on the knob. "Do you even want me to come?"

I wonder if this is why Olivia doesn't want to have kids, because her own mother was such a fuck up. Or if it's because of me, because she already feels like she raised one kid.

"Don't be stupid," I say.

She smiles, shakes her head and turns to go.

16. Thursday (Olivia)
On my lunch break, I checked my messages and was disappointed to have none.

I multitasked, eating the sandwich I'd packed that morning as I drove to the mall. Charlie was easy to shop for. She appreciated shiny colorful trinkets: scarves and earrings, glass vases and scented candles, hand-made pottery and wind chimes. She liked the idea that the object made you think of her; that alone gave it value and meaning. I was the opposite. I hated *tchotchkes.* Give me a book by my favorite author or a practical object I mentioned needing or something I pointed out as particularly lovely. Prove that you know me, that you care enough to pay attention. Or don't waste your money.

Charlie was not as hard on people as I was. I should have seen that as a virtue. And usually I did, but now it had me scouring the aisles of Forever Twenty-One for a gift that would outdo my mother.

Every August, Charlie and Carmen went back-to-school shopping with Mrs. Rodriguez. Those first few years without my mother, there were things I couldn't do myself, like drive, and by the time I could, this was a tradition between the three of them.
And yet, somehow, I'd never felt this sort of competitiveness with Carmen's mother. Lydia had always felt like a supplement to the family we'd become when my mother left. Her existence was a relief, not a threat.

I ran a hand along the rack of blouses, searching for a feeling. Something with a distinct and unusual texture, so soft it felt like a liquid.

What was it Greg had told me? I didn't stop being who I was no matter who my mother suddenly chose to be. Something like that. What made it especially hard to swallow was how desperate Charlie seemed for my mother to step back in. I'd had no idea. All those years, she'd quietly settled for what I had to give while needing so much more.

I went back to work empty-handed.

Rick started texting me before I'd gotten in my front door. I ignored him at first, hunting Oscar down. He was sleeping in his favorite cardboard box and I didn't wake him.

I punctured the cellophane on my frozen dinner and stood in front of the humming microwave as it rotated on its carousel.

I probably shouldn't have given Greg my number. Technically, he wasn't my patient, but if someone at work had seen us getting a beer the other night, it might have looked funny. There were rules at the practice against dating patients. Not that it had been a date. Socializing. Fraternizing. They'd warned us about it in school.

My phone chimed and I snatched it from my pocket. Rick had sent a picture from the Bosnian place on Oracle. We often went there on Thursdays, enjoying the quiet of the nearly empty dining room. It let us talk to each other and relax in a way we never could in a noisy, hectic chain restaurant. We convinced ourselves the place was busier on Friday nights, raking in the cash it needed to stay afloat. We preferred restaurants that weren't crowded, but that often meant our favorite places went out of business on a regular basis.

Lately, though, our meals had been pretty quiet. I couldn't remember the last time we'd had a meaningful conversation, one where it felt like we were on the same page.

"I'm already making dinner," I texted back. The timer beeped and I pulled the cellophane away from the tray, burning my thumb in the steam. I stirred the contents and returned it to the microwave for another two minutes.

We had worried especially for Alisah's – an odd location in a building that looked more like a motel, bad signage, inadequate parking (or perhaps sadly, adequate, but limited.) But the food was great. It was run by a family. The patriarch often gave us off-menu specials: the creamy mushroom chicken breast he'd made for his wife and son just that night.

I took my dinner to the couch to eat in front of the television, "like a grown up" as Rick would say. Anything that required cutting had to be eaten at the table. Everything else was couch approved. Rick had grown up in a family that was required to eat at the table together. In my family, I'd been the one to create such rules. So what felt like a transgression for him felt more like hypocrisy to me. Either way it was a taboo.

I found a documentary on Netflix about the current crisis on the Tucson border. When the geniuses in Congress had decided to build a wall, all they'd managed to do was shift the crossing to the most treacherous of borderlands in Arizona. There was still no shortage of undocumented immigrants; the only difference was that now the ones who didn't make it died horrible deaths of exposure in the Sonoran desert. Hundreds each year.

Oscar took the corner, squawking a greeting. He seemed disgruntled that I'd snuck in the house without his noticing. He stopped at my feet – he wasn't allowed on the couch while I was eating – and pretended obliviousness. He couldn't be accused of begging when he was looking away. He just happened to be nearby if I needed assistance.

Another picture came in of Bosnian style kebabs. The cubed chicken I was eating resembled something I'd find in one of Oscar's cans. I tried not to look too closely, focusing on the television. My Spanish wasn't good enough to ignore the subtitles.

Each year the US government threw more millions at the problem, but there weren't fewer immigrants because that was never the intention. Before, worker programs satisfied both sides. The US got their cheap labor; the migrants got to return to their families with what they'd earned. Now, they had to stay in the shadows and send money home. Meanwhile, a very select group of Americans got rich by creating the illusion that Mexican workers were unwelcome.

My dinner was likely the result of that labor. When I finished eating, I set the plastic tray on the floor and Oscar wasted no time licking up the gravy. When he'd polished it to a shine, he hopped up into my lap and allowed me to scratch beneath his chin as he squinted at the ceiling.

I didn't get another text from Rick until eleven. "Been drinking. Pick me up?"

I knew what he was doing. It had gone this way before. I found my keys in the kitchen and headed out.

I pulled into the lot and parked beside Rick's truck. He climbed out and waited for me to unlock the passenger door.

"Your buddies just left you here?"

He slid in beside me. "They knew I had a ride coming."

Of course they did. I backed out of the parking space.

"You got someone to get you to your car in the morning?"

He smirked. "You can."

"I'm not staying over."

"No?"

"Uh-uh."

He sighed and leaned against his door. "Suit yourself," he mumbled. I was relieved that he didn't argue the point. I could handle a little sulk.

I rolled down the windows and lost myself in the loud rush of air. It was in the nineties during the day, but had cooled so much that my arms were quickly covered in goose-bumps. In the darkness, I was unable to keep my bearings by placing the mountains. The Santa Catalinas dissolved into the night and made the landscape generic. We could be anywhere.

"You ready for Charlie's party on Sunday?" he asked as I turned on my blinker and took the right to his apartment complex.

I groaned. "Not really."

"She called me yesterday to be sure I knew I was still invited, in spite of…"

"How I might feel about it?" I laughed and shook my head. My hair was a tangled mess from the wind.

"How do you feel about it?"

I pulled into a spot in front of his building. "Well, you'd hardly be my least favorite guest."

"Now there's a compliment."

"Sorry. My mother will be there."

"She mentioned that too."

I leaned my head back and closed my eyes.

He covered my hand with his. "Are you okay?"

I turned my hand over so our palms were touching. Otherwise, I didn't move. We sat like that for several minutes in the cool quiet. At the other end of the complex, car doors slammed and laughter carried. When Rick leaned in and kissed me, I let him. It felt inevitable. His hands were in my hair and then sliding down my back. I pushed against his chest, a gentle pressure. *Enough.*

"We need to let each other go," I said.

"I don't want to let go. Maybe we're supposed to be together," he said, and it was the *maybe* that lost his case. If he'd been sure, he might have convinced me. I was worn out with my own uncertainty.

I'd grown up with the same stories as all the other girls: the fairytales about finding true love. In spite of the up-close view of my parents' failure, these stories still occupied space in the back of my mind. I was pretty sure they were bunk, but what if I was wrong?

It was the same with God. I was pretty sure it was bunk, but what if I was wrong? I lived my life so it shouldn't have mattered. If it turned out there was some grandfatherly figure looking out for us all, I could hardly imagine why he'd turn me away at the Pearly Gates.

But the soul mate fairy tale depended on the other, bigger fairy tale. In order to believe in them, you had to believe in the concept of the soul.

"We're going to be friends for the rest of our lives," I said. "But we can't start being friends 'til we stop this in-between nonsense."

Rick rubbed the back of his neck and looked out the windshield. "We're gonna be friends for the rest of our lives?"

"We are." I wanted to reach out and touch him, but I knew better. I put my hands back on the steering wheel, ten and two. "You're going to marry some totally kick ass woman who likes sci-fi and cartoons and children. And she won't be threatened at all by the friendship with your weird, loner ex-girlfriend."

He shifted his weight, bumping shoulders. "Can we have a wild affair in our forties?"

"No, dummy. You're married."

"What if I'm divorced by then?"

"Such an optimist."

He took a deep breath, held it, let it out. "So this is it then?"

I squeezed the wheel. "Yep."

"You really don't want to come in? Just one more time?"

I shook my head. Personally, I couldn't think of anything sadder than making love and knowing it was the end. Clearly, men were built differently.

"But, last time? I didn't even use my best moves."

"Sure you did."

"Nah. I got better moves."

I laughed at that. "You do not. I know all your moves."

He made a face.

"They're good moves. I'll remember them fondly." And I would. That last time, I'd been on top. When he came, he'd held me tightly against his chest and cried out. Then, he caressed my back and thighs, bringing me along. He never left me behind.

He got out of the car, shut the door and leaned into the open window.

"I love you, you know."

"And I love you."

"So should I go to the party?"

.

17. Friday (Charlie)

After my morning classes, I meet Carmen's mother in the driveway in front of her house. I park on the curb; she's got the side of the minivan open and she's loading it up.

"Hello, Mija," she says to me. She's wearing Capri pants and a pink fanny pack around her generous middle. Inside, she will have lip balm, band-aids, aspirin and a million other forgettable necessities. "Do you need to pee before I lock the house?"

"No. I'm good."

She points the clicker at the van and the door slides shut. She darts to the front of the house, locks up and hurries back. "I packed us a lunch. You ready?"

I nod.

"Then let's hit it." She runs around to the driver's side and is already buckling her seatbelt when I climb in next to her.

She backs out of the driveway and begins listing the contents of the little cooler sitting behind us. "I know. Food, food, food. The irony's not lost on me." She shakes her head. "I'm bracing myself for the family counseling. It's always the mother's fault."

"That's not true," I say. "When is family counseling?"

"I'm not sure. I know they want to keep the focus on Carmen for a while at first. They don't allow distraction: no TV or internet, no cell phones."

"Wow. We could invent a news story and she'd never know. Wanna?"

She laughs. "You're so bad." We pass a homeless man on the corner and her mouth forms a straight line. His skin is like leather, the color of red clay. We merge onto the highway and she shifts in her seat. "No, you are bad," she says, as if she's just remembered. "You are in trouble with me."

"I am?" My smile falters and I feel queasy.

"With everything that's going on with Carmen, I haven't had a chance to talk to you about your little trip to Las Vegas. You gave us all quite a scare."

"I know. I'm sorry."

She continues to scowl. "You can't treat family that way. I don't care how angry you get at them. That sister of yours? She'd die for you. Your father too. We don't all get that." She has always talked with her hands. The way this translates when she's driving is that her left hand grips the wheel while her right hand makes up for its motionlessness with wild swooping and pointing.

"I know." I stare at my lap.

"Carmen and Jorge and me too. We're your family. You don't just take off and let us think you're dead. It isn't right."

I nod. She's being harder on me than my dad was.

"You're an adult. You don't need permission to go places, but you still have obligations to the people who love you. That makes you lucky. You can't take that love for granted."

"I'm really sorry."

"I don't need you to be sorry. I need you to never do it again."

"I won't."

"Good." The car slides back into the slow lane. "Now tell me about your mother. What has she been up to all these years?"

I'm relieved for the change in subject. When I tell her about my mother's alcoholism and recovery, she groans and shakes her head. Jorge's brother is a recovering alcoholic; she knows something about this struggle, seems sympathetic.

"She's coming to the party on Sunday," I tell her.

"Wow. Is your dad okay with that?"

"Yeah."

"And Olivia?"

I shrug. "She knows."

Carmen's mother nods slowly and it's clear she has noticed that I didn't answer her question.

Carmen makes choking noises as her mother hugs her. Her eyes bulge at me and she grins: I'm in on the joke. I return a half smile. Although often it feels like Carmen and I are two physical extensions of the same person, this is not one of those times. My mother's embrace could never feel like a burden. I can't even imagine it.

Carmen leads us to the patio outside. We sit at a round table; the umbrella jutting from the center adds to the feeling that we're at some kind of a resort. I expect to flag down a waiter for some iced teas. Menus, at least. What would they serve at a treatment center for eating disorders?

"Are you going nuts without your phone?" I ask. Carmen conducts her life on that thing. I've missed her middle-of-the-night text messages.

"Actually, they keep us pretty busy. Everything's very scheduled." Carmen's wearing red jean cut offs and a loose black t-shirt. Her sandals are quickly cast aside and she pulls her bare feet onto the chair, hugging her knees. "They won't let me do any school work, though. I'm going to fall so behind."

"Don't worry about that," her mother tells her. "You have the summer to catch up."

"I know." A strand of Carmen's dark hair falls across her face and I wonder why she doesn't push it back.

"I've already spoken with all your professors," her mother says.

"Oh, that's just great." Carmen closes her eyes and presses a hand to her forehead. "Did you tell them why I'm here?"

Carmen's mother hesitates before going with the truth. She nods.

"Mami!" Carmen throws up her hands. "Couldn't you have just said *hospital*? I don't want everyone thinking I'm crazy."

"They don't think that, Mija. They were very understanding and sympathetic."

"Great. So they feel sorry for me? God!"

"You're going to miss the rest of the semester. What should I have told them?"

"Nothing! I never asked you to talk to them. It wasn't your place." She buries her face as she hugs her knees more tightly to her body.

Carmen's mother looks stung. The three of us sit quietly for a long moment. The sky is bright blue and cloudless. "I'm going to find the restroom and let you girls talk."

Carmen's slender arms jut out from the sleeves in her shirt, skin and bones. She looks no different from last week, but I'm so used to seeing her this way, it's hard to judge. It has only been a few days. I wait for her mother to disappear around a corner before I speak. "Your mom's just trying to help."

Carmen lifts her head and frowns at me. "I'm gone for three days and you're already on her side?"

"No. There aren't sides."

She rolls her eyes. What I was supposed to say was this: *I'm on your side. Always.*

"I can't take the way she's looking at me," she says. "Like I'm such a disappointment."

It's hard to believe we've been watching the same woman. "Carmen, your mom loves you so much."

"All of a sudden you're an expert on mother love?"

I flinch.

"Sorry. That sounded less mean in my head."

"It's fine."

"I'm just on edge. You know, they weigh us everyday but they never tell us the number. And they sit with us at meals and write down any ED behavior."

"ED?"

"Eating disorder."

I nod. "They have a really good reputation so they must know what they're doing."

I can see by her face that I've failed again, taking their side. It's so hard to walk that tightrope between supporting and enabling. Like, I want her to know I will be there for her no matter what. I will love her when she's hurt or sick or miserable. But I don't *want* her to be miserable. I don't want to make it so okay for her to be miserable that it's all she can ever be.

I give it another shot: "I know it's hard, but you just have to trust them. You have to get better."

"I want to," she says, her voice thick with tears she's struggling not to shed. "I'm trying."

I can never let her know how scared I am for her or she will stop telling me the truth. One of us always has to lie and I know it needs to be me.

"Good," I say. "That's all you can do right now. That's a lot."

When Carmen's mother returns to the table, we stick to safer topics of conversation. When they hug goodbye, Carmen makes no protest.

In the car, we buckle our seatbelts. Mrs. Rodriguez starts the engine and fusses with her mirrors as if they could have shifted since we got here.

"She didn't mean to be so hard on you," I say.

She sighs. "I know. She's just scared." She turns to me then and I see the tears in her eyes. "You girls are so loyal to each other. It's admirable to see." She smiles. A tear catches in her lashes and she blinks it away. "But you need to know when to draw the line." She reaches across and takes both my hands in hers, squeezing hard. "You can't be so loyal you're willing to watch each other fall off a cliff without letting anyone know you need help."

I let this sink in. This time, I really hadn't known Carmen was in trouble. I hadn't been around to notice. But there have been other times. I've always prided myself in my secret keeping. This feels like more tightrope walking.

Mrs. Rodriguez is studying my face, waiting for a response.

"Okay," I say and she lets go of my hands, turns to look out the windshield and throws the car in drive.

She turns on the radio to something twangy. In Arizona, it's this or the Spanish stations. We don't say much else until she drops me at my car two hours later.

"Pick you up for church on Sunday?"

"Without Carmen?"

"Jorge and I are still going. She needs our prayers while she's away. Unless you don't want to go."

"No, I do."

"7:45."

"I'll be ready."

When I get home, I call my mother. The phone rings one too many times and I start to panic. I've already told everyone she's coming.

"Charlotte."

I let out the breath I've been holding. "Hey."

"What's up?"

I flop back across my bed and close my eyes. "I kinda had a rough day. Went to see Carmen at the treatment center."

"How is she?"

"I'm not sure. I worry she's fighting it, you know? Doubting the process."

"That's hard." She sighs. "I think you have to brace yourself because it doesn't always work the first time, but that doesn't mean it won't work eventually. If it's anything like addiction, she has to want to get better for herself."

"I really want it. Can't that be enough?" I force a laugh.

"I wish it could."

I realize that what I want is for her to just tell me everything will be okay. As if I'm a child. I rub my temples with forefinger and thumb. "I know all I can do is be here."

"Well, you can do more than that. You can encourage her, let her know you believe in her. I think sometimes we fail when no one's expecting us to succeed. That's what a support system is for."

"Did you have that?"

"Not at first. I think that's part of why it was so hard."

"You have it now, though. With Ben? And with me."

"I do."

I hug myself and warmth fills my chest. My eyes flutter open. "Were you drinking when you left us? Was that why you left?" It's easier to ask it without having to see her face.

She's quiet, but I know I haven't dropped the call because I can still hear her breathing. "Yes and no," she says at last. "I don't think I recognized the drinking as a problem yet, even though it clearly was. I hid a bottle of vodka in the laundry room, in the cabinet above the washer and dryer. I'd drink while you girls were at school, during the day. But at the time, I thought the drinking was the solution, not the problem."

"The solution to?"

"Feeling overwhelmed and unhappy, like I didn't fit, like I couldn't be who I really was."

"Because of us?" I pinch my eyes shut and press the cell to my ear.

"No, Charlotte. None of it was because of you."

I sigh. Of course she has to say this and yet I still take comfort in hearing it. There are more questions, maybe there will always be more questions, but first things first. "You're still coming, right?" I try to say this casually, but I'm afraid it sounds like begging.

"Ben and I are driving down tomorrow. We'll stay with his sister, Amy, on Saturday and then we'll see you at the party on Sunday."

"I can't wait."

18. Saturday (Olivia)

Oscar came to the patio door with that scowl on his face, looking at me like *there you are*, like I was in trouble. After a moment, he seemed to acquiesce to the idea that this was what we were doing now and he jumped into the chair beside me, curled into a ball and went to sleep.

I was reading the latest novel by Julia Glass. She was delving deeper into the lives of characters who had been on the edges of her earlier work. I liked this idea: we are all peripheral characters in someone else's story and every peripheral character is the lead in their own.

I had to lay a towel across my hips or the sun would turn the rivets in my jeans to instruments of torture. This was my favorite thing to do, but in just a few more weeks, it would be too hot to read in the backyard, even in the shade.

Yesterday, after work, I'd wandered through the shops on Fourth Avenue. Still clueless as to what to get Charlie for her birthday, I bought several things, charging them all with my credit card. I'd select something tomorrow and return the rest before they billed me. For now, the options were strewn across my bed: a sparkly clutch, a book about traveling in Europe, a wall mirror framed with orange mosaic tiles. Earlier, as I looked over the collection, I felt bereft; none of them seemed right.

A bird's nest had been blown from the tree the night before. Its contents were scattered. I would have expected twigs and grass but these were city birds; they made do with what they could find: a piece of black rubber tire, a twist tie from a sandwich bag. I thought it was depressing at first, the way humans were wrecking their quaint little bird lives, encroaching on their habitat with ours. But it was also kind of inspiring; they were resilient.

I sat in my father's back yard while the cake cooled on the kitchen counter. Yellow cake mix from a box – Charlie's favorite. I would lather it with chocolate frosting from a can – also her favorite. On the table in front of me, there was a tall glass of iced tea and the kitchen timer.

The glass door slid open and Charlie stepped outside. She was wearing jeans and a black tank top that revealed her red bra straps. "Tanning?"

I turned my palms to the sun. "Feels nice."

"Watch out or they'll start asking you for your papers."

I frowned. A few years back Arizona had become known for its anti-immigration policy that allowed the police to ask to see proof of citizenship for anyone they had reason to suspect might be undocumented. Anyone brown. They'd never bothered Charlie, as far as I knew.

But how far was that?

Charlie was always making these comments, implying I wasn't Mexican enough. Because I didn't speak Spanish or go to church, like she did. She'd even insisted on having a *quinceanera* when she turned fifteen.

"You don't have cake pans at your place?" She sat down across from me.

"Nope. You're the only person I ever make cake for." I also didn't want to have to worry about driving over with a cake on my front seat, arriving to the party with it mashed and mangled. "No sampling before the guests arrive."

"I'm not a child."

I sighed. It felt too depressing to explain that I was joking. "So, you're still mad." It wasn't a question.

"Me?" She shrugged and glared across the table. "What do I have to be mad about?"

"Look, Charlie, I should have told you. When you were eighteen. But when you were twelve, you didn't need some drunk—"

She sprung forward in her seat and slapped the table. "You didn't even know she had a drinking problem until I told you. And she was not some drunk! She was my mother. What the hell did you know about what I needed?"

"You were having a hard time that year. Struggling in school. I didn't want to rock the boat."

"Did it ever occur to you that I wasn't doing well because I was motherless?"

"I was motherless at your age," I reminded her.

"You had her for twelve years. I only had half of that."

As if it was a competition. As if it could be whittled down to that.

"At least you had me," I said. "I know it's not the same."

"No. It's not the same."

It stung, but I tried to let that be okay. Charlie was entitled to her feelings. "I thought I was doing what was best for you. If I was wrong, I'm sorry. I am."

She looked deflated then, like she hadn't expected me to apologize. Now she had to wrestle with forgiveness when she wasn't ready to give up the anger that fueled her.

The timer went off. "Frosting." I explained and got to my feet. I stood over her for a moment, thinking to hug her or pat her shoulder, but in the end I just went inside.

When the cake was frosted, I wrapped it in cellophane and left it in the fridge. Charlie was in her room by then and I didn't bother saying goodbye. In the car, I returned Greg's message, inviting me to dinner.

"Still up for some company?" I asked.

"I'm making tilapia. Do you like fish?"

"You know what? That sounds awesome. What can I bring?"

Greg said to bring nothing, but I couldn't do that so I picked up a bottle of wine. Last night I'd pored through the handbook I'd received when I started working at Desert Oasis. It was very clear on the issue of dating patients. But when it came to friendships with another therapist's patients, it was silent.

Greg answered the door wearing jeans and a pale blue polo shirt. His wavy dark hair fell into his eyes and he tossed it back, smiling crookedly. "Olivia, hi. You look nice."

It was such a *date* thing to say. I felt myself flush as I looked down. I was wearing the same clothes I'd had on all day.

I stepped inside and followed Greg into the kitchen. "The fish is in the oven," he said, pulling a drawer open and retrieving two wine glasses. He turned and took the bottle from me.

"I know nothing about wine," I admitted. "I just thought the label was pretty."

He laughed and held the bottle out, looking it over. "I think you're right. That's as good a criteria as any." He found a corkscrew and handed me the glasses once he'd poured. "Let's go outside while it cooks. It's so cool."

He led me out to the patio. It was closed in by a low wall made of stucco. I walked to the edge and looked up at the sky. "Not many more nights like this."

I handed him his glass and he took a sip. "They'll be back. Just a few months."

I agreed and we were quiet, watching the sun set over the mountains. A lizard scurried across the cement floor.

"How was your day?" he asked.

I groaned.

He lifted his eyebrows. "That good?"

"I had another difficult conversation with my sister. It seems to be the only kind we have these days."

"Ah. Sorry to hear that."

"I just don't understand how can she be so mad at me but she can forgive that woman."

"Being mad at you is safe. She knows you're not going anywhere."

"I suppose." I tried the wine. It was sharp and sweet, cold. I set my glass on the wall and turned toward him. "How's PT?"

"It's fine."

"Does Phil have you on a home exercise program?"

He tipped his head. "Let's not."

"What?"

He shrugged. "I'm not your patient, Olivia."

"I know."

"I have plenty of people in my life who treat me that way. I'm covered."

I raised my arms in surrender. "Okay. Sorry."

He shrugged like it was no big thing, smiled. "I know you're used to taking care of everyone else, but maybe you should let someone take care of you once in a while."

I bristled.

"You know, for the next twenty minutes or so," he added quickly, looking at his wrist, at a watch that wasn't there. He placed his hand over mine where it rested on the wall and although he continued speaking, I couldn't hear his words, just the thrumming of my heartbeat in my ears. I looked down at his large hand obscuring my slender fingers. I slid my hand out from under his, stepping back.

Greg stopped talking. His face looked ashen.

"I can't," I said.

He nodded. "I'm sorry."

"I should go."

"Oh, God, no. Let's just eat. There's no reason—"

"I shouldn't have come. It wouldn't look right."

"It's just dinner. I like talking to you."

"I like talking to *you*."

"I have no problem just being friends. Let's just forget I tried to hold your hand." He attempted to laugh it off, but his face was red.

"I think I've given you the wrong impression," I began. I was losing my S sounds in the hiss of the cicadas and felt like I was lisping.

"Not at all. You're not interested. It's fine."

"No, I mean if you think I'm not interested, I've given you the wrong impression."

Greg hesitated. An uncertain half-smile twitched at his lips. "Go on?"

"You're a patient." I looked past him, at the mountains gathering shadow, at our wine glasses, abandoned on the wall. The metal patio table with its empty chairs and closed umbrella. Anywhere but in his eyes.

"That's what you're worried about?" he asked.

I folded my arms. "My job is important to me."

"Of course it is. I'm sorry. It just hadn't occurred to me." He pressed his fingers to his forehead. "There must be a way around it?"

A breeze rustled the palm fronds overhead. I leaned against the wall, rubbing my arms. "Could you ask Phil to refer you to another office?"

Greg contemplated the ground. "It was quite difficult to find an office that takes my insurance."

"Oh."

"Olivia, I'm kidding."

"Oh." I smiled slowly. "You're very funny."

"Yes, I am."

In the kitchen, the timer beeped.

He reached for my wine glass and held it out to me. "You staying?"

I took it. "Yes, I am."

Chapter 19 (Sunday) Maria

Ben kisses my forehead and mumbles something I'm not awake enough to hear. Gradually, the noises from the kitchen get louder: dishes and silverware, the nonsense ramblings of Amy's youngest which veer toward screeching, followed by an adult shushing.

The guest room is so fancy. Ben's little sister seems to be trying too hard. She's already his favorite person in the world; there's no need to impress him with fresh cut flowers. The plush chair in the corner holds a half dozen decorative pillows in assorted shapes and sizes. I will try my best to return them to their proper places when I make the bed.

For now, I look at the ceiling and pretend I'm giving Ben time to talk to his sister alone, something he hasn't been able to do since we got here yesterday. I roll over and bury my face in the pillow. Ten more minutes.

Last night, I met Ben's mother at dinner. She had long white-blond hair mixed with silver and I didn't like to think that this prim older woman was nearly as close to me in age as he was. Ben's brother couldn't make it, as usual, something that he understands but struggles to accept. Everyone has their own limitations when it comes to forgiveness. Ben and I have watched each other learn to live with that.

When you fall for someone in the program, there's no need to have the conversation where you let them in on your baggage. Do you give it to them on the first date or the third? All at once or in dribs and drabs? We had each other figured out from the first night. By now, I know his stories like I know my own. He'd shared them first in that musty church basement, later in my living room with more details and tears.

Ben had grown up hating his abusive alcoholic father and was horrified to find himself repeating the pattern in his early twenties. After that girlfriend left him, he'd begun drinking in earnest and when he found a drunk who gave as good as she got, he married her. When she got pregnant, he assumed she'd get an abortion. Instead, she got sober and found Jesus and they were no longer a match. At his worst, he threw a glass and it shattered against the wall. A sliver of that glass had hit his baby daughter in the soft pale baby fat of her leg as she perched on her mother's hip.

He'd left the next morning and as much as he wished he could say he got sober after that, it took him three more years. In that time, his wife remarried and he gave up his parental rights so the new husband could adopt. He understood what's lost when you choose alcohol over your child.

We'd spent months talking intimately, falling in love slowly. But nothing had happened until I got my year chip. I was following the program to the letter and he knew. No relationships for the first year. He'd taken me out that night to celebrate and we both knew what was happening without ever having to talk about it. He'd slept over every night after that.

Until Charlotte arrived.

I slip out of bed and go to the bathroom to brush my teeth, put on a bit of make-up. Although it feels like we've known each other forever, some things are still new.

What you're supposed to say is that if you had your life to do over again, you wouldn't leave or, at the very least, you wouldn't change a thing because the result was bringing your children into the world. Only a monster thinks otherwise and only a complete moron says it out loud.

But the truth is, if I had it to do over again, I never would have married Roger, my daughters wouldn't exist, and I wouldn't have lost more than a decade of my life drinking to punish myself for not being the woman I'd promised to be.

The tricky thing is that leaving my daughters wasn't the mistake. For me, having children was the mistake. I'd never wanted to be a mother, but I wanted to be Roger's wife and that came with giving him children. I knew that much when we got married. Someone else would worry about paying the rent on time, get to the bottom of the weird clunking sound the car made. Or just buy a new car. Roger was a dentist. I didn't need to compare the prices on canned vegetables at the grocery store or spend the last week of every month eating a potato for dinner and trying to ignore the gnawing in my stomach as I slept. We actually ate out on a regular basis. He'd slide his credit card into the billfold without even looking at the total. We'd walk to the parking lot with his arm around my shoulder. I was his and I was safe.

It was a price I thought I could pay. It was my choice, my mistake.

Of course, I can't explain any of that to Olivia or Charlotte. For them, their births were not mistakes. It's that something can be a mistake for me, but not a mistake for them, that both things can be true *at the same time,* that's what makes the truth so complicated.

The pro-lifers are always insisting an aborted fetus is a tragedy because given the chance it might have grown up to cure cancer. They never seem to think what that girl might have done with her life if she hadn't been saddled with children she didn't want. Maybe *she* would have cured cancer.

And this is the way humans pass the buck eternally. Because I have made nothing of myself – just getting through the day without drinking is my version of success – but I'm a mother so all is not lost. I don't have to make something of myself or contribute anything meaningful to society because they might. Or they might just have children of their own and pass the buck for another generation.

We're just kicking the can down the road.

But you can't say that out loud. So you don't. And you try not to think about changing the past, since you can't anyway.

I drive to the coffee shop by myself. Migrant workers stand in a gas station parking lot. No rest, even on the Lord's day. The mountains are crisply visible against the blue-blue sky, so unlike the mountains in California which are hard to see through the thick orange- brown smog.

The door chimes as I enter. I tried to get here early, but he's already sitting at a table in the corner, looking at the screen of his phone. He puts it down as I approach.

"Roger, hello."

"Maria." He doesn't stand or smile or offer to shake my hand.

"I'm just going to get a coffee," I say and I slide into the line, grateful for the reprieve. I wait for my name to be called while I try to calm my breathing. My hands are shaking as I stir in the cream and sugar.

I take the seat across from him and smooth my palms against the front of my skirt. He looks good, but I don't say that. He's become rugged with age. "Thanks for seeing me."

He nods and says nothing.

My coffee is too hot to drink, but I don't trust myself to remove the lid without spilling. I hold it tightly with both hands. "I thought if we saw each other first, it would be less awkward at the party."

"So you said on the phone."

He's not about to make this easy. Well, why should he? "I'm sorry if my being there is going to be hard for you."

"It was important to Charlotte and she's important to me."

"She's such a great girl."

"I know."

Of course he does. "What I mean to say is thank you. For taking care of them when I couldn't."

"It's not something I need thanks for. Certainly not yours."

"Okay." He's wearing a pale green polo shirt. There's a loose thread at the collar. "Well, can I bring something to the party? Chips? Soda?"

"We're all set."

I nod. After thirteen years, this is the conversation we're having.

"So is this enough? We've seen each other?" he asks.

I don't know what I was expecting. That we'd hug and cry? That he'd let himself ask me why and I'd come up with an answer that could make him understand?

I nod, unable to find my voice. When he's gone, I rip the lid from my cup and watch the steam rise.

Roger was the kind of man who thought life was what you make of it, and for men like Roger, it was.

At the beginning, he thought we were the same, neither of us having parents, building a family from scratch. He'd had a lifetime of devoted parenting before his mother and father left this earth without intending to. His mother's only job had been to take care of him. She cooked his meals and did his laundry and helped with his homework. When he was sixteen, his parents bought him a car. They paid for his education. He was their only child, their pride and joy.

My mother drowned in a river before I was two. I don't remember her and it wasn't until after Olivia was born that it occurred to me it hadn't been an accident. What was she doing in a river at night, by herself? Once my mother was gone, my father lost interest in being a family man. He left me with my *tia*, his sister, in Arizona. She already had so many kids, he probably thought she wouldn't notice one more and mostly she didn't. I think he sent money back, at least for a while, but I never heard from him again. I was raised among an ever-expanding flock, lost in the shuffle.

Our house in Nogales was a temporary stop for extended family making the crossing, on their way to Texas or California with the clothes on their backs and a distrust of indoor plumbing. They'd put their used toilet paper in the wastebasket.

It was hard to feel close to anyone in a family so large and shifting. My cousin Nina is the only one I'm still in touch with. Two years older than me, she used to ride on the back of motorcycles and I wanted to be just like her. When I was seventeen, I slept with my aunt's boyfriend and got kicked out of the house. Nina understood something that even I didn't understand at the time: I hadn't wanted it, not really.

I got a lot of things I never wanted, and I'm not blaming anyone for that. They were my decisions, my mistakes, and I have to own them, sorry or not.

I left my aunt's house with four scratches on my left cheek.

I'd grown up speaking Spanish, but I hadn't set foot in Mexico until I was seventeen. It was Nina's idea to go see my *abuela*, who I'd never met. It was that or Nina's couch. She drove.

I stayed there for a month and fell for a local boy who had no intention of going to America, one of the few. I considered settling down in this village, staying close to my grandmother. She was the first member of my family to make me feel precious. Her hugs stole oxygen and replaced it with something even more vital.

When I told her I was thinking of staying in Mexico permanently, she told me I was a fool. There was no life to be had here. If this boy was serious about staying in the village, we'd be too poor to feed ourselves. Whatever children we had would cross the border as soon as they were able and never come back. These were lessons she had learned.

My father's father had crossed legally in the sixties, part of a worker program created to replace the labor of Americans fighting in wars overseas. When that program was terminated, the Mexicans who didn't go home, like my grandfather, became *illegals*.

Over the next few years, my father and his siblings joined him. My grandmother did not. She didn't want to leave her parents and by the time they passed on, she was too old to make the crossing. I suspected, though she never said, that my grandfather had another woman by then as well. He still sent money back; she didn't think she'd survive otherwise.

That night, my grandmother got out her photo albums and traced her finger over the faces of children she'd lost to America. In the morning, she helped me pack my small bag. I was no longer welcome to stay.

She probably thought she was doing right by me, but I kicked myself for letting my guard down, for thinking I could matter to someone in that way only family really matters. I swore I'd never again give someone the power to reject me, and, for a very long time, I never did.

Olivia opens the door. It's the same as it was all those years ago except Ben is standing next to me as I hold his hand more tightly than could possibly be comfortable. Olivia is wearing dark jeans and a sunny yellow tank top. Her honey brown hair is pulled into a pony tail. Behind her, there's a crowd in the kitchen.

"Come in," she says, all manners, stepping back and motioning with her arms. She's Vanna White, her face frozen in an interpretation of the pleasant hostess. We follow her inside.

Gifts are stacked on the island in the kitchen. I add my box to the pile. It's a silver bracelet with Charlotte's name engraved. I had it professionally wrapped at the jewelry store and they topped it with curlicues of lavender ribbon.

Charlotte isn't in the kitchen. Olivia does not make introductions, instead presenting herself as useful to a woman at the stove.

Ben begins to exchange names and handshakes with the people seated at the table. Jorge Rodriguez has gotten round in the middle, but still has a thick head of hair. He shakes my hand and says it's nice to see me again and I am overwhelmed by this tiny gesture of peace. I take his hand in both of mine and squeeze. To keep from crying, I turn to the next figure at the table. Mrs. Carver has not changed one bit.

"Brave of you to come, dear," she says with a sour look on her face. I'm holding her fleshy hand, leaning in and wondering if I've understood her correctly when I hear the slice of the sliding glass door opening. Charlotte stands in the threshold.

"Charlie!" Everyone shouts in unison and my face flushes. She steps into the kitchen and hugs me hello, then pulls me outside to introduce me to her friends.

After awkward hellos, the young people wander to the far side of the yard while Ben and I sit at the table on the patio. It's sunny, but not too hot. Charlotte pulls soda cans out of a cooler nearby and sits down with us, asks about our drive.

The glass door *whooshes* open and Olivia steps out with a bowl in each hand and a bag of chips pinned against her hip with an elbow. She sets everything on the table in front of us, salsa and guacamole, and introduces us to the empty-handed young man who has followed her outside. Rick. She calls him a friend, but there's some other energy between them that makes me wonder if they're newly dating.

To my surprise, they both sit down and it's the five of us.

"Carmen's mom makes the best guacamole," Charlotte says and she leans forward, digging in.

It's nice to have something to busy ourselves with, to occupy our hands and fill our mouths. We murmur and nod. Yes, the guacamole.

Roger nods a hello, his hands full of hamburger patties and buns. Rick joins him at the grill, to help. Ben asks for the restroom and Olivia offers to take him. She's rising from her chair but he says no; he won't get lost.

Ben leans in to kiss my cheek; he looks in my eyes. "You got this," he says, and he sounds so sure that I believe him.

Olivia settles back into her chair. A silence swells. My chip snaps in the bowl of salsa and I have to get another chip to fish it out.

"Do you like Nevada?" Olivia asks and I'm distracted from my pursuit of the broken chip.

We proceed to talk about nothing. Geography and weather and driving routes. Television shows and how lately they're better than movies. We compare the way sizes run in various clothing stores and the travesty of fashion trends repeating decades best forgotten. It's superficial small-talk that avoids any emotional landmines. Maybe someday we'll go deeper, but for now we wade safely in the shallows.

I look past Charlotte and she assures me Ben is fine, probably got trapped by Jorge, he's a talker. When Ben returns, we're laughing and by the time he's sat down I've forgotten why.

When the girls were small, I measured time in manageable blocks. The weekend was a trial to get through; school on Monday was the light at the end of the tunnel. When Olivia came home from school, I counted the hours until bedtime, when I could sneak off to the laundry room alone and slip into bed once Roger was snoring.

Summer break was a horror; it stretched out forever. There was never a reprieve. It was like trying to hold your breath for three months, impossible.

I'd create projects or trips, something to look forward to. I pressured Roger to take me somewhere, anywhere, and I'd settled on Las Vegas. I got it in my head that everything would be different once we came home from that family vacation. We'd be different. I rode the gondolas with the girls and then again just the two of us at night, desperate to capture a feeling. I thought everything would be ok if only we did it right.

But we came home the same people to the same life. The next thing was the kitchen renovation. I searched for tile and pendant lamps like my life depended on it. It took months and when it was complete, I was elated. For a few hours. Then Roger left his coffee cup in the sink and the girls' breakfast bowls and school papers accumulated on the new island and suddenly it was just a kitchen.

I thought it would get better when Charlotte started first grade, but it really didn't and by April I was dreading the summer when they'd both be home all day and there'd be no way to hide or get a moment to myself.

I went to Nina's when I left and that's when the drinking really got out of control. I didn't want to think about what I had done and there was no longer any reason to stop.

There's a lull in the conversation that starts to make me itchy. Olivia sits back with her arms crossed, staring at her lap. Charlotte sips at her can of soda. Ben slides his arm across the back of my chair.

Suddenly, Olivia looks directly at me. "So were you drunk that time you came to the house all those years ago?"

Charlotte gasps. Ben squeezes my shoulders.

"I was sober."

"But it didn't last."

"No."

"How do we know it'll last this time?"

"Olivia!" Charlotte slams down her soda and looks prepared to knock her sister over.

"It's okay," I say with a calm at odds with my heart rate. "It's a valid question."

Charlotte sits back in her chair, scowling. Olivia waits for my response, expressionless.

"The answer is that we don't know. We never know. As they say: one day at a time."

I think I see Olivia suppress an eye roll. She nods instead, a slow bobbing of her head.

"But this time she has us," Charlotte says. "A support system. That's what makes it different." She leans forward and reaches for my hand across the table.

I smile for her. Her fierce hopefulness is something precious and admirable. "That's the plan."

"Well, good luck," Olivia says and it sounds almost sarcastic until she adds: "Really."

I thank her. When Rick approaches with her hamburger on a paper plate, she goes inside with him to eat.

There are burgers and tamales and mac salad and sopapillas and brownies. Ben fills a plate for each of us, which prevents me from having to approach Roger at the grill. There are other guests eating in the kitchen or sitting on the raised flowerbeds on the far side of the yard. I remember planting some of the shrubs there.

When I finish eating, I need a smoke. I stand and make explanations in a low voice.

"I can get you an ashtray," Charlotte offers.

"Oh, no. Too many people," I say. I hate smoking among non-smokers. It makes me feel dirty and self-conscious, defeating the whole purpose of having such a release.

"But you're coming back, right?" Charlotte asks, her eyebrows angled for an impending disaster.

"Of course. Of course," I say and I pat her bare shoulder.

Ben follows me out through the kitchen, past the refrigerator I selected back in another life when I thought it mattered.

Outside, I lean against the car and light my cigarette. Ben is an ex-smoker, quit long enough that it doesn't even bother him to smell it, or so he says. Twice, I've used the patch to quit and it worked well: for nine months and two years, alternately. I've thought of switching to the vapor, and that's probably what I'll try next, but for now I'm not ready to give up the ritual of it. It's my last vice.

"How're you doing?" Ben leans against the car beside me; our arms are touching.

"Everyone calls her Charlie," I say and I think of the bracelet.

He's quiet for a moment, thoughtful. "Sometimes my mom calls me Benjamin. Only her. It's special."

"Yeah?"

"Yeah. If she wanted you to call her Charlie, she'd have said so."

"Okay," I say and I hope he's right.

I think of her worried face as we were leaving. As much as she wants to believe she's forgiven me, she hasn't. For the rest of my life I must continue to apologize; it would take my whole life and then some to make it up. Charlotte is bottomless; her forgiveness is conditional, she's always testing. Olivia may have no use for me, but I no longer feel the anger coming off of her in waves. She has let it go. She worries about me only in terms of how I might affect her sister. Otherwise, I am of no consequence.

I understand it. I accept it as a natural result of my actions. But in many ways it was easier when I was alone. I didn't have to prove myself over and over. It's exhausting.

When we return to the patio, Lydia and Jorge have moved outside. They're sitting at the table and the girls are standing across the yard, in separate little semi-circles. They're both so beautiful. So tall. They look deliberately distinct, but you can see they're sisters. It's clear despite attempts to differentiate with superficial styling. They both have Roger's long nose, my dark eyes.

I take my seat next to Ben. He and Jorge disappear into a conversation about water harvesting. I didn't even know Ben had an interest in this.

Lydia leans toward me. "How long are you in Tucson?"

"We'll drive back tomorrow."

"Would you like to meet for coffee in the morning? I have some photos of the girls."

I cover my mouth with my hand and look away, blinking. I don't trust myself to speak, so I nod my head.

20. Sunday (Charlie)

From across the yard, I watch as my mother and Carmen's mother sit at the patio table, talking politely. Suddenly, my mother clasps her hand over her mouth and turns away. I can't imagine what's been said and also I can imagine several things.

In three long strides, I'm by my mother's side. I touch her shoulder. "Is everything okay here?"

She looks up at me and smiles through tears. She blinks and they're gone and I have to wonder if they were ever really there. "Of course," she says and she slides an arm around my waist.

Carmen's mother stands. "Jorge and I are going to head home," she says and she hugs me. She squeezes me tight, releases, then squeezes tight again. "This one is from Carmen."

She goes inside with Jorge. I know they will haggle about leftovers with my father in the kitchen, like always. He'll insist they take some home, they'll refuse, and he'll pretend frustration.

I sit at the table with my mother and Ben. "Are you having a good time?"

"We are."

"Someone brought fireworks for later."

"Oh, I'm not sure we can stay much after dark. I don't want to keep Ben's sister up late."

I want to argue but I know I can't keep her here forever. Things would get awkward at bedtime. Part of me wants her to go now, before anything bad can happen. Her presence feels precarious; it could take a turn at any moment and then she'd never come back. There have already been a few close calls.

Olivia is across the yard with Rick. She throws her head back, laughing, and I wonder again why they have to break up. I don't understand any of it.

"Why don't I get the gift?" Ben offers.

"That's okay," my mother says quickly. "She can open it later."

"No, no, get it." I nod at Ben, ignoring my mother's squirming discomfort. He kisses the top of her head and goes into the house. "It's my birthday," I shrug when she turns to me.

"Yes, it is," she agrees.

Ben returns with a small box. The paper is a metallic silver and the purple ribbon has been curled by a perfectionist. I pry it free without tearing it and tuck it into the pocket of my shirt so it cascades out like a corsage. I scratch at the tape and unfold the paper carefully. Lifting the lid of the white box, I see a silver cuff and when I tilt it, it catches the light and shows my name carved in script on the inside. It reminds me of the one I'd found beside her bed when I went snooping, only hers had been gold.

I slip it on and hold my arm out for appraisal.

"Everyone calls you Charlie," my mother says. She seems embarrassed.

"It's okay. I like that you call me Charlotte." And I do. It is so rare that someone uses the name I was given at birth. It feels intimate.

Ben leans in toward my mother, winking at her.

I slip the bracelet off again, balancing the weight of it in my palm, running my fingers along the edge, feeling the grooves my name makes in the metal.

"You have to stay for cake," I tell them and they nod, convinced.

In the bathroom, I reapply lip-gloss in the mirror. I can hear voices from outside. As long as we use the swamp cooler, we have to leave a window open in every room. When we shift to AC next moth, we'll seal the house. For now, conversation drifts in, but I can't make out what they're saying.

When I left, my mother and Ben were sitting at the table together in a safe little bubble. My dad and Rick were talking to two of my friends from school. Olivia was in the kitchen, wrapping up leftovers. The party is dwindling.

Yesterday, Olivia apologized for my perception that she'd done something wrong. It was right up there with the "I'm sorry you *feel that way*" apology which doesn't take responsibility for your behavior; it just expresses your regret for the other person being crazy. Olivia said she was sorry *if* it had been wrong to keep my mother from me since I was twelve. Olivia heard the apology, checking it off her to-do list; I heard the *if*.

I press my pinky into the groove of my top lip, removing the excess gloss. I run my tongue over my teeth and shoot an exaggerated grin at my reflection.

On the way back through the house, I find Dan sitting alone in the living room, looking at his phone. I sit next to him on the couch. “Boring party?”

He laughs. “Nah. Just checking my email.”

“It’s okay. You don’t have to stay. Lydia and Jorge left.”

“You trying to get rid of me?” He elbows me in the ribs and I let out a giggle.

“No way, man. You’ve got the fireworks.”

“Exactly. You gotta be nice to me.”

“Ah.” I lean back. “Did you get cake?’

“I got a corner piece,” he boasts, sitting up straighter and thrusting his chest out.

“Good job.”

He nods and looks at me over his shoulder. “Are you having a fun birthday?”

I sigh. “Sure.”

“But?”

“It’s hard.”

“Without Carmen?”

I nod. That’s a big part of it.

“Me too.”

He’s leaning forward, talking to the carpet. I reach out and pat his back. I’m trying to think of something to say, something reassuring about Carmen – how she’ll be okay or she’ll be home soon – when he turns to me. He starts to lean toward me with his mouth partially open and his eyes partially closed. It’s happening in slow motion but also at an unfathomable speed. I strike out at him, horrified and perplexed, smacking him in the throat with the base of my palm.

“What the fuck?” I shout.

He bends over, coughing.

“Seriously. What is wrong with you?”

He sits up, apologizing.

“Carmen is in *treatment* right now,” I say.

“I know.”

“And now I have to tell her that her boyfriend’s a total loser.”

“You don’t have to tell her.”

“Of course I’m going to tell her.” I shake my head at him.

“I was just, like, confused.”

"Confused? About what?" I stand up. "You're so gross. That's what you are. Get the fuck out of my house."

He sits there, slumped forward, and rubs his hand over his stupid bald head. He screws his eyes shut like he's wishing to undo the moment with time travel. When that doesn't work, he gets up.

I slam the door behind him, stomp to my room and slam that door as well.

Olivia hardly knocks before pushing the door open. "What's going on?" And then, before waiting for an answer: "You can't just hang out in here. There are people outside."

"I just need a minute. God!" I flop backward onto my mattress.

"What happened?" She's holding a green kitchen towel in both hands, twisting it.

"Dan tried to kiss me."

"He *what*?"

I throw my arms up in the air like I've proven my point: I'm someone entitled to a moment alone. *See!*

She sits down on the edge of the bed and lays the towel over her knees. "Are you okay?"

"Yes," I huff with annoyance. "But why are men so horrible?"

She laughs then, the concern deserting her face. "They're not all horrible," she says.

"Like, he thought I'd sacrifice a life-long friendship just so I could make out with some dumb meathead?"

Olivia laughs harder. "Maybe boys are horrible. Give it a few years." She puts her hand on my knee and squeezes.

I pull my leg away and she folds her hands in her lap.

"Dad's a good guy, yeah?" she says.

"That's one."

"And Rick."

"You're dumping Rick."

"I'm not *dumping* him." She scowls at me. "We're not breaking up because he's a bad guy."

"Fine." I like Rick.

"And this new guy I'm dating. Well, it's early, but I don't think he's horrible either."

I raise an eyebrow at her. Under usual circumstances, I'd press for details, but I don't want to give the wrong impression. I'm still too angry at her to let her win me over with juicy boy stories. I cross my arms with resolve. I will not ask about her personal life

Olivia gets to her feet suddenly, leaving the kitchen towel on the bed behind her. "What's this?" She lifts the catalogue from my nightstand and holds it up. The colored photo of happy college students under a banner. The University of Arizona.

"It's not for me," I say and I look past her, not wanting to see her disappointment.

"Okay," she says, slowly. It's a question.

I sit up and snatch it out of her hands. "I got it for Carmen."

"Oh."

She waits for me to say more, but I don't. Instead, I think about the way she grilled our mother about her sobriety. I place the brochure back on my nightstand and sit with my feet under me.

"You didn't have to be so hard on her before," I say.

Olivia turns her back, pressing a finger to bend the slats of the Venetian blinds. "Someone did and it wasn't gonna be you."

"Don't you think she's suffered enough?"

She hesitates and it feels like she's actually considering this. "Maybe," she says finally. She stops pretending to look out the window, turns to face me. "We should probably get back to the party."

I groan. "I'm gonna have to tell them there won't be fireworks." I swing my legs off the bed.

"It'll be okay."

I feel like I've been waiting a long time for her to tell me that.

The sky is a light blue, bright and honey-tinged and surreal. In moments, it will deepen to gray as the sun disappears. We stand in the street: my mother and Ben, Olivia and I. It's time to say goodbye.

As I hug my mother, I force myself not to ask when I'll see her again. Olivia steps backward onto the curb, holding her elbows tightly and looking at the ground. Ben gets in the car first and then slower, more hesitant, my mother gets into the passenger's side.

They drive away. The tail lights pulse at the end of the street, the right blinker. I lift my hand and wave as they take the corner.

Olivia steps off the sidewalk and puts an arm around my shoulder.

“This isn’t just happening to you.”

I feel stung. “I know that.” I try to pull away, but she holds on.

“No,” she says. “I mean: I’m here with you.”

I understand. It wasn’t a rebuke; it was a statement of solidarity. We’re in this together. We turn and go back to the house, secure in the knowledge that my father will be there, waiting.

Acknowledgements

Sometimes writing can feel like a solitary endeavor but I've been lucky enough to find that it doesn't always have to be. Years ago, I stumbled into a writer's community called Authonomy.com and the writers I met there have challenged and supported me through the years. I'm especially grateful to the talented members of the Women's Fiction Critique Group run by Gail Cleare, critique partners like Mary Vensel White, and too many "beta readers" to mention by name.

In my real life, I have amazing friends and family who inspire me, give me pep talks when needed, and help me get the details right. I'm talking about Reed Nava, Sean Flanagan and Wendy O'Rourke (among others). These people have shaped my work and my life and both are better for it.

About the author

Katie O'Rourke was born and raised in New England, growing up along the seacoast of New Hampshire. She went to college in Massachusetts and now lives in Tucson with her boyfriend. She likes to read good fiction in the sunshine of her back yard. A hybrid author, this is O'Rourke's third novel. She is always working on her next book.

A note from the author:

Thank you for reading my book! I would love to hear from you. You can email me at **katiewritesfiction@gmail.com** or check out my website: **www.katieorourke.com**.

I certainly hope you enjoyed reading Finding Charlie. If you liked it, please check out my newest release, Blood & Water. My books have overlapping characters, so even though they aren't sequels, they're all connected and give readers a chance to see some familiar faces.

Thanks again.

All the best,

Katie

Praise for Blood & Water:

"Delilah is leaving her cheating boyfriend and she has nowhere to go except the home of her brother, whom she hasn't seen since their mother's funeral five years before. David is a single father trying to manage his teenage daughter, and he's not exactly pleased when his wayward sister shows up. From the opening of this absorbing novel, as Delilah nurses a black eye and ransacks her apartment, trying to decide what she can't leave behind, I was fully along for the ride. The widening ensemble of characters each have their own voice, their own journey to define family and home. *Blood & Water* is Katie O'Rourke's most compelling and heartfelt novel to date, a story about family—past and present, predetermined and chosen—and the deep veins that keep them connected."

~ author Mary Vensel White

Delilah

It isn't yet dawn as I ransack my apartment for things I can't leave behind. The list is surprisingly short.

Handfuls of clothing stuffed into a duffel bag. My laptop. An awkwardly-sized cardboard box full of nostalgia, the only things I'd allowed myself to take from my parents' house after my mother died. I wrap both arms around it, hefting it onto my hip as I cast my eyes in nervous darting circles, contemplating what doesn't make the cut. The futon. The microwave. Sheets and towels and curtains. I leave it all.

Everything fits quite easily in my Mini Cooper, the box and the duffel bag smooshed together on the backseat like sleepy children apprehensive of the spontaneous road trip. I go back to lock up, remembering to take a pale blue scarf from the hook just inside the door. I drape it over my fleece, which I zip up to my chin on the way back to the car. I slide into the front seat and turn the key. It starts right up – nothing like nightmares and old movies, where people can never leave in a hurry when they need to. Everything goes smoothly. Leaving is easy. As I pull out of the lot, and my apartment building gets smaller in the rearview, my breathing slows. I'm certain I won't miss any of it. I wonder why I never thought of this before.

I feel no attachment to material things. I take some degree of pride in that. Near the end of her life, my mother asked me to take her antique furniture. She had an oak dresser and nightstand that were a set and she didn't want them separated. She was dying and she was worried about keeping the furniture together.

After the funeral, there'd been an estate sale. I don't believe in an afterlife so I don't believe my mother is upset with me or proud of me or looking out for me.

Dead is dead.

The cardboard box contains twelve file folders that hold report cards and artwork and essays from every year I went to school. If I looked closely, I'm sure I'd find my SAT scores. I haven't looked closely, though. I saved a shoebox full of loose photos, but I haven't looked closely at those either. When I first lifted the lid in the basement, my throat started closing. I replaced the lid and set it aside. For later. Whenever that is.

My mother died five years ago, six months after being diagnosed with lung cancer. She'd never smoked. My father had smoked, though he quit before I was born. He'd died before her diagnosis. A heart attack we hadn't seen coming. She'd just begun to shake off the most crippling parts of her widowhood when she got the news that she wouldn't need to get used to living without him after all.

My father's death was sudden and shocking and devoid of the opportunity to say goodbye. It was terrifyingly fast: the fear in his eyes, his twisted face, the ambulance sirens too late. My mother's death was miserably slow, an endless terror with a million goodbyes until there was nothing left to say and nothing left to do but wait for the guilty relief when it was over.

Tucked into a corner of that box, wrapped in a checkered kitchen towel, are their wedding rings and her quarter carat diamond in yellow gold, the only jewelry my mother owned.

As I wait at the intersection on the way to the highway, remembering my favorite frying pan with grooves in it that made burgers look like they'd been grilled, I see a police cruiser in my rearview mirror. It turns into the parking lot of my apartment complex and I take a right on red.

Made in the USA
Middletown, DE
15 September 2021